The Sign of the Calico Quartz

Sweetbrier Inn Mysteries
Book One

Jan Drexler

Jan Drexler

Published by Swift Wings Press
Keystone, South Dakota

Print: ISBN-13 979-8-9861378-0-3

Cover design by Hannah Linder
www.hannahlinderdesigns.com

Edited by Beth Jamison

To my dear husband,
who loves the Black Hills
as much as I do.

Soli Deo Gloria

One

I dropped my suitcase on the front porch of the Sweetbrier Inn and pushed on the door lever. It didn't budge.

Seriously? An inn with a locked door? I rang the bell.

Setting Tim's carrier on the porch next to my suitcase, I hugged myself to ward off a sudden chill. Flakes drifting through the air caught my eye. Snow at the end of April. Great.

Tim meowed at me from his carrier, demanding release. He stuck one black paw through the wire door.

"Don't worry. You'll have your freedom soon enough."

I rang the bell again, holding the button down until the electronic ring had sounded three times. Barking erupted from somewhere in the building. I shivered. My light knit wrap over its matching t-shirt wasn't warm enough for snow.

Through the door's window I saw movement, then a three-inch gap appeared.

"We aren't open yet. You'll have to try one of the motels in Rapid City."

The voice was rich, striking, and male.

"I'm Rose's niece, Emma Blackwood. You must be Wil Scott, her business partner."

The door opened a little wider and I caught a glimpse of a sandy-haired man about my age. His face was ruddy, like he had been out in the chilly weather.

"Rose said you would be coming today, but you're early. She didn't think you would be here until around five." Wil opened the door wider so I could step into the foyer with Tim and my suitcase.

"I caught an earlier flight. She isn't here?"

"She went into town to purchase supplies for the season opening this weekend. She'll return any time."

The barking grew louder, then a corgi came rushing toward us, his nails scrambling on the polished wood floor. I knelt to greet him.

"This must be Thatcher." I held his smiling face between my hands and rubbed his ears. His tri-color markings included black lines around his eyes that made him look like he was wearing spectacles.

"That dog." Humorous disgust filled Wil's voice. "He got out of his crate again. I keep telling Rose that she needs to put a lock on that thing."

"He's just a smart puppy." The dog's eyes half-closed as I scratched his chest. "And the cutest thing."

"Cutest brat, you mean." Wil closed the door and picked up my suitcase. "As long as Rose is at home, he's fine. But as soon as she walks out the door, he's a holy terror."

"He can't be that bad." I watched the dog approach the door of Tim's cat carrier, caution in every step. "It looks like he and Tim might get along."

"Tim?"

"My cat." I indicated the crate. Thatcher's nose was stuck through the wire door and his tail was wiggling.

"That dog doesn't get along with anyone."

His smile belied his gruff words. It was just a bit crooked. One a girl would die for. I grabbed Tim's carrier and stood up again, dusting my knees with the other hand to avoid his gaze. Maybe some girls would fall for a grin like that, but it would be a long time before another guy caught my eye, cute as a teen heartthrob or not.

"Rose said she had a room for me?"

"Ah, yes." That voice again. As rich as chocolate pudding. With the timbre my dad would have described as a radio voice. "She said you'll have the upstairs suite while you're here."

Wil took my suitcase and led the way up the open stairs that turned behind the reception desk. As I approached the landing halfway up, I got a good view of the ground floor library. A grand piano filled the open space between it and the dining area.

"Did I see on the website that the inn has seven guest rooms?"

"Six rooms are available this year." Wil set my suitcase at the top of the stairs. "Five up here and a sixth one downstairs. Your suite is the seventh room."

A comfortable lounge filled the center of the second floor with guest rooms opening off the common area. A hall extended to the right with a door marked "private" at the end.

Wil turned to the left and opened another door. He stood back so I could enter first, then followed with my suitcase.

I stopped just inside the door. "Oh, how lovely."

We were in an L-shaped sitting room with a sectional sofa placed in the center, providing a walkway around the perimeter of the room. Through an open door on the left I caught a glimpse of a bedroom, and in the short end of the L was a mini kitchen. Wil opened a set of French doors on the opposite side of the sitting area and stepped out onto a balcony. He didn't seem to notice the snowflakes drifting through the air.

"This suite has a private deck." He turned that boyish grin on me again. "The Agatha Christie is the best room in the inn, other than Rose's apartment downstairs."

"The Agatha Christie?" I suppressed an urge to look around to see if Hercule Poirot was observing me.

"All the rooms in the inn are named after roses." That quirky grin appeared again. "It was your aunt's idea. Her suite is the Evangeline."

I glanced at the plaque on the open door. The painted rose was pink with glossy green leaves and the name was inscribed above the flower.

"And what is yours called?"

He stepped back into the room and closed the French doors with a firm click, his back to me. "My apartment doesn't have a name. Technically, it's separate from the inn."

"This one is gorgeous, no matter what its name is. But I could have stayed in one of the other rooms." As an employee, I certainly didn't want to claim a premium room and cut into the profit margin.

"Don't worry about it. Rose's orders." Another crooked grin. Forget the teen heartthrob. He was definitely an Indiana Jones type. The younger version. "I'll let you get unpacked. The key is on the ottoman there," he indicated a cushioned square tucked into the L of the sectional, "and supper is at six. I'm fixing crab soup, so I hope you like seafood."

"I love it. I hope this snow doesn't delay Rose. I'm looking forward to seeing her."

"Snow?" He looked out at the deck again. "Oh, that. This light dusting won't bother Rose. She'll be here." He nodded toward the window. "That's her car now."

Leaving Tim in his carrier, I followed Wil and Thatcher back down the stairs and into a passageway behind the reception desk. Through an open doorway on my left, I caught a glimpse of a professional kitchen and a whiff of the crab soup Wil had promised, and on the other side of the hall was another door that revealed a utility room of some kind. Wil opened the door at the end of the passage leading to the spacious garage. Rose was just getting out of a forest green Range Rover.

"Emma," she said, opening her arms to embrace me in a close hug. Then she held me at arm's

5

length. "You've changed since the last time I saw you."

"I was eight years old then." I looked into the face that hadn't aged much over the years. Only a few extra smile lines and silver hair. "I hope I've changed since then."

"How long have you been here? I thought I'd be home in time to greet you properly with a cup of tea and time to chat."

I went to the back of the SUV where Wil was opening the back hatch to reveal a load of paper goods and food. "Just long enough to take Tim and my suitcase upstairs."

"Then let's get these groceries inside and have that cup of tea." Rose grabbed a stack of cotton bath towels. "You can tell me all about the last twenty-five years in person instead of through a telephone line."

As Wil disappeared into the inn with a stack of boxes, Rose stopped me with a hand on my arm. "I'm so glad you're here." Her voice was low, her words meant for only me. "I really need your help with the inn."

Concern washed over me. "Is something wrong?"

She shook her head. "Nothing specific, just a few quirks here and there. I've been feeling my age this winter and I don't want the inn to suffer because of it. And my memoirs take up more time than I thought they would."

"I can't imagine how much time it takes to write a book," I said as I picked up a warehouse-sized package of paper towels. "And you are not that old."

Rose smiled as she led the way toward the garage entrance into the inn. "I may not seem old, but time is a persistent thief. You're here now, though, and that's all that matters." She turned into what I had called a utility room, but it turned out to be a large pantry with a laundry center at the far end. She dropped the towels on an island countertop in the center of the room. "We open in two days, and we are completely booked through the middle of August." Her face grew serious as she faced me. "I need you, Emma. I hope you'll like it here."

I gave her a hug, pushing down the concern that reared its head again.

"Don't worry. We'll make this the best year ever."

"Not bad for the first day of the season, is it?"

I jumped at the sudden voice in my ear. "Wil, stop that. You know I don't like it when people sneak up on me."

He grinned as if he thought it would send my stomach into a tailspin. It might have yesterday, but after working with him to prepare the inn for today's opening, he was more of an irritating brother than a possible romance.

"You'll just have to get used to it, because it's fun to watch you jump."

I kept my next comment to myself. If he thought he was the king of witty banter, he was wrong. It hadn't taken long for me to discover that his boyish good looks often extended to his maturity level, as well. But I had to admit he was a fabulous chef. The crab soup had been exquisite.

"Hey." Wil nudged me with his elbow and leaned on the buffet next to me. "You need to lighten up. Life at the Sweetbrier Inn isn't as stressful as it is in the big city."

I rubbed my temples, then focused on the guests grouped around the dining room munching on their afternoon refreshments. As much as I wanted to, I couldn't relax until I was certain every visitor was enjoying themselves.

Watching Rose chat with her guests, I saw a woman in her element. As we had gotten reacquainted the previous evening, I had caught my aunt's vision for the inn. I had been used to working for a hospitality corporation who treated the budget like a gold mine, eking out every penny to bolster the bottom line. But Rose thought differently.

"I don't have to make money, dear," Aunt Rose had said with a laugh when I had asked her about the budget. "The inn is here to serve guests who are looking for a comfortable place to stay. Our purpose is to provide that for them, not to get rich."

Her shoulder-length silver hair was caught in a bun, but other than that she looked like she was only a few years older than my own thirty-three-and-a-half. I tried to ignore the half.

"As long as we don't lose money, I'm not concerned about the profit." She had leaned forward in her chair, her slim form enclosed in a cozy-looking shawl. "Life is meant to be enjoyed. To be lived to its fullest."

As I watched the guests enjoying their tea and scones on this first afternoon, I had to agree with Rose. I would gladly give up the corporate life for this relaxed atmosphere if Rose was thinking about keeping me on for more than this summer. The conversation was light, Thatcher was safely in his crate in Rose's apartment, Tim had made himself at home in my rooms upstairs, and the scones were delicious.

"What's this I hear about a gold mine?" one of the guests asked, his voice booming above the conversations around him.

I smiled, thinking of the mnemonic I had come up with to remember his name: Seeker Sam. Sam Nelson and his wife Nora were in the Black Hills looking for gold. They had booked a guide for a solid week of tramping through the Hills, panning streams, exploring old mines, and hoping to strike it rich.

"That's right," Montgomery Reynolds answered. Mysterious Montgomery was my name for him. His cultured British accent seemed to be hiding his real purpose for visiting the Sweetbrier. "There's an abandoned gold mine near here, just up the road." He smiled at Rose, sitting next to him at one of the round tables scattered throughout the large room. "I came here to research that mine."

"I'm afraid there is no gold there, though," Rose said. "The name of the mine is Graves' Folly. It didn't pay out more than a few dollars for the original owner back in the late eighteen-nineties and drove him into bankruptcy. And then a mine accident killed a few of the miners and Old Mr. Graves closed it up for good."

"What about uranium?" Sam asked. "I heard that's the next big boom in these hills."

"Then you heard wrong," Rose said, her smile gone but her voice even. "If there is any uranium, it isn't worth the trouble of mining it."

"Trouble?" Sam said. "If there's a large enough amount, it could be worth millions."

"No amount of money could make up for the destruction of the natural beauty of the Hills and the danger to the residents."

Wil grunted.

"You don't agree?" I kept my voice low, my question only for Wil.

"Uranium will make us all rich once people like your aunt see the light."

"But is it worth it if it destroys this beautiful area?"

Wil frowned and motioned for me to be silent.

"That doesn't bother me," Montgomery said, continuing the conversation, and I'm sure I saw him wink at Rose. "I'm not interested in gold or uranium." He sat back in his chair and raised his voice so all the guests could hear. "I'm writing a book, you see. It's on the history of mining in this area."

Wil snorted softly, still hanging around by my right shoulder. "As if there has never been a book written on the history of this area."

His voice had risen slightly, and Annie Smith and her husband Roger glanced our way. They were both teachers from Nebraska on their honeymoon in the Black Hills. I smiled at the couple as they sat at the table near my post just inside the dining room and Annie smiled back before turning toward Rose at the table next to theirs.

"Is it true that Paul Peterson is supposed to be here?" Annie asked.

"The ghost hunter?" Montgomery asked. "I should hope not. I was hoping for a quiet week of research."

"You are right," Rose said. "Mr. Peterson and his assistant are expected at any time. But I hope we will all treat them just like any other guest of the inn."

Roger whistled. "Just think of it, a famous television star, here in the same inn where we're staying."

Sam snorted. "I would hardly call the man a television star. He hosts one of those reality shows, doesn't he?"

Roger took Annie's hand as he leaned toward Sam. "We're big fans of 'Paul Peterson: Ghost Chaser.' Never miss an episode. In fact, during the last season he nearly captured a ghost in an old mine in Colorado. You remember it, don't you dear?"

He went on talking, but only Annie listened to him while Sam said something to his wife Nora, and Montgomery's attention was drawn by the third person sitting at the table with him and Rose.

"I think it's fascinating that you're writing a book." This was Clara Benson, Rose's long-time friend who booked a two-week stay at the beginning of the season every year. "I would love to hear about it."

Montgomery blushed and lifted his teacup as he looked toward Rose for help. I didn't blame him. Of the two unattached ladies close to his age, Rose was the more attractive one of the two. Clara's middle-age plumpness had settled in for the long haul, and her hair was a mousy grayish-brown frizz, as if it had seen too many home permanents and dying sessions. But Clara had her own charm, and Rose loved her.

The front door opened with a bang, driven by the wind and the force of the personality who entered. I slipped behind the reception desk to check the couple in, but everyone knew who they were. The woman stopped at the desk as her companion strode into the dining room, removing his overcoat and trademark red scarf with a flourish that reminded me of a movie star from times past. My mind supplied the mnemonic Pretentious Paul, although I doubted I would need it to remember his name.

"Good evening, ladies and gentlemen," he said, dipping his chin in what could have been taken for a bow. "Paul Peterson, at your service." He struck the classic pose from his television show, his right arm extended toward the darkest corner of the room, and said, "Let's chase some ghosts!"

Everyone laughed at the well-known tag line.

Roger shifted in his seat as Annie kept a restraining hand on his arm. Paul noticed and strode over to him.

"Are you, by any chance, a fan of my show?"

"We both are," Roger said, his voice rising in excitement. "Aren't we, Annie?"

As Paul turned toward Annie, his face froze as if he had seen, well, a ghost. The look was gone in a second and he turned toward Roger again.

"You'll be here all week?" he asked.

Roger stood and shook Paul's hand. "Yes, we will. In fact, if you need any assistance in your ghost hunting venture, just let Annie and I know." He blushed and stammered. "We- we're j-just amateurs, but we can't pass up an opportunity to work with the great Paul Peterson."

Montgomery groaned. "Stop making such a big deal about the quack."

My head started to throb. Our enjoyable afternoon was threatening to split at the seams.

"A quack, sir?" Paul didn't look at Montgomery but scanned the rest of the faces in the room, then focused on Rose. "Dear lady, you wouldn't strike such a blow as that, would you?"

"I wouldn't dare to say anything," Rose said, smiling first at Paul and then at Montgomery. "Mr. Peterson is here to explore the old mine, too. You should have a lot in common with each other."

"I'm researching the mine for historical information." Montgomery sniffed and sat back in his chair. "I doubt we would find much common ground."

Rose reached across the table and touched Montgomery's sleeve. The action immediately brought all his attention to her.

"Can you tell us anything about that old mine?" she asked.

I had to give Rose credit for knowing how to ease the tension in a room.

Montgomery shook his head. "I only know a few bits and pieces, which is why I'm spending the next week here. I hope to find records or surveys that would help me with my search. I don't suppose you know of any residents of Paragon that would have something like that hidden away in their attics?"

"I have just what you need right here. The mine is on the land owned by the inn, and I've collected all the old papers related to this property. I keep them right here in our library." Rose stood. "I'll show you where they are so you can browse through them at your leisure."

As Rose and Montgomery walked past the piano and into the library just off the dining room, the other guests returned to their conversations.

I sighed, relieved, and reached for the guest register. I opened it to the page listing the inn's reservations.

"You must be Mary Walters," I said to the woman who had been standing on the other side of the reception desk, watching Paul with a worried frown on her face.

"Yes, Paul's personal assistant. I'm sorry if he disturbed your gathering."

"Not at all." I handed her a pen to sign in while I ran her credit card. "We've all been waiting for you to arrive, and Mr. Peterson's entrance didn't disappoint."

"Our reservations for next week are confirmed, as well?"

I clicked the computer screen to show the next week. "Yes. The entire inn is reserved for your staff and crew. Is that when you'll be filming the next episode of your show?"

"That's what Paul has planned," she said with a little laugh. "He likes to spend time on location planning how the episode will be filmed, then bring the crew in. You know, after we locate the ghosts."

"Do you always locate ghosts?" I asked.

"Of course." Ms. Walters smiled. "Do you know any ghosts who would pass up an opportunity to appear on television with the great Paul Peterson?"

I smiled back, then glanced into the dining room. Mr. Peterson was holding the guests spellbound as he entertained them with a story.

"Ms. Walters, I can help you carry the bags upstairs."

"Oh, thank you." She stuffed her gloves into her coat pocket. "And call me Mary, please. Paul and I prefer people to use our first names."

"Of course," I said. "Your rooms are upstairs, in the far corner of the lounge."

I took the largest suitcase, an expensive-looking leather and canvas monstrosity, and led the way. Thankfully, it was attached to a luggage trolley with large wheels that handled the stairs easily. I opened the doors of the two rooms and handed the keys to Mary.

"Make yourselves at home. These two rooms are connected by a pass-through door for your convenience. We will continue serving tea and scones in the dining room until five this afternoon. Breakfast starts at seven o'clock each morning and is available until nine o'clock."

Mary walked into the Albertine room with her wheeled bags. "Paul wasn't sure he wanted to stay at a bed and breakfast, but when I saw your chef's credentials, I knew we wouldn't want to miss his cooking."

"Yes, Wil does a wonderful job. He's a perfectionist and never serves a dish you wouldn't die for."

"I'm looking forward to it."

I closed the door and let a happy smile break my professional image as I crossed the lounge, straightening magazines on the side tables as I headed toward the stairway. One thing I had learned in my years in the hotel business is that some guests could be tiring while others were a delight to host. It seemed that Mary was in the latter category. Mild Mary fit her perfectly.

A meow sounded from somewhere behind me in the lounge.

"Tim?"

The inky black cat purred and padded toward me across the room, threading his body through table legs on his way. He stretched himself up my leg and I took him into my arms, scratching the one white patch on his furry chest.

"What are you doing out here?"

He butted his head against my chin as I walked toward the door of my suite. I was sure he had been sleeping on the couch when I left just after breakfast this morning. I hadn't been back to my suite since then.

I unlocked the door and opened it wide enough to tuck Tim inside, but in the dim afternoon shadows I saw something on the floor between the door and the sofa. I switched on the light.

A shoe? I looked closer, putting Tim on the floor as he squirmed in my arms. A man's shoe.

I closed the door so the cat wouldn't escape again and stepped farther into the room. Another shoe was next to the sofa, the rounded toe propped against the chaise. Brown leather and well-worn. Dried mud clinging to the edges of the soles. Not tucked neatly under the edge of the couch, like my shoes would have been, but random. Casual. As if someone had sat on the ottoman and kicked them off, toe to heel. First one, then the other. Tim sniffed the nearest shoe with a delicate nose touch. He jumped away in a sideways dance and ran behind the sofa.

What was a pair of men's shoes doing in my suite?

A tray sat in the center of the ottoman with two wine glasses. An empty bottle lay on its side on the couch.

I shook my head. Another joke of Wil's. Why couldn't he stick to old stand-bys like rubber cheese in my sandwich? And really, coming into my private room was going a bit too far.

When I bent down to pick up the shoes, Tim yowled from somewhere near the window.

"What's wrong now?"

I left the shoes where they were and leaned over the back of the sofa.

A man was sleeping on the floor, on his side, facing the wall. I glanced at his feet. Red socks. No shoes. At least that mystery was solved.

"Hey!"

He didn't move. Was he passed out? Drunk?

And why was he in my room?

I circled the sectional thinking I would shake him awake, but when I touched his shoulder he rolled from his side onto his back, his eyes open and staring at the ceiling. I leaned over him.

"Are you okay?" I touched his shoulder again. "Hey, are you hurt? Sir?"

That's when it struck me. He wasn't asleep.

Two

I'm not sure how I survived the next half-hour.
As Wil took the empty scone trays back to the
kitchen, I cleared away plates and teacups from the
tables, my fingers so cold I nearly dropped a tray full
of dishes. Pasting a smile on my face, I tried to
pretend everything was normal. The guests must not
think anything was wrong.

Sam looked at his watch. "We have reservations
for dinner, Nora. We'd better be going."

They headed up to their room, followed by Roger
and Annie. Paul had wandered into the library while I
was upstairs, and now he came out of the alcove with
Rose and Montgomery.

"I'm sure these maps will add new interest to my
book," Montgomery was saying. "I'll have copies
made and get them back to you as soon as I can."

"There is no hurry." Rose walked with him to the
foot of the stairs. "I hope they will be a help to you."

Paul pushed past Rose and looked over
Montgomery's shoulder at the papers he was carrying.

"I say, old boy," he said, mimicking Montgomery's
British accent, "you wouldn't mind making a copy of
those for me, too, would you?"

Montgomery shrugged Paul away. "If Rose agrees,

I can do that."

"I have no objections." Rose smiled at the two men, but I saw the pinching at the corners of her eyes. "I'll see you both at breakfast. Remember, the front door of the inn is locked at eleven o'clock tonight. Call the inn's number if you're going to be late."

"Don't worry," Mary said, coming down the stairs to meet Paul. "We'll be back soon after supper." She picked up a restaurant guide from the reception desk and leafed through it as she followed Paul out the door.

"Rose." I put my hand on her arm. "I have something to tell you."

As she turned toward me, Sam and Nora came down the stairs dressed as if they were planning to party the night away. Annie and Roger were behind them, their casual clothes a contrast to the other couple's. Finally, Montgomery descended the stairs, pulling on leather driving gloves.

"Good night, ladies," he said.

"That's all of them," Rose said as Clara joined us. "It was a successful first afternoon, don't you think?"

"Except for one thing."

"What's that, dear?"

I glanced at Clara. If Rose treated her as more of a friend than a guest, then I could, too. I took a deep breath.

"There's a man in my room. He might be dead. I think."

The police arrived within two minutes of the time Wil called them. I mean, him. It turned out that the deputy was one of Paragon's leading citizens and was at home when he got the call.

He was tall, rangy, and stern with sunglasses in his shirt pocket and a pistol on his belt. He removed his cowboy hat as he entered the inn and set it on the reception desk. Silver threaded through his wavy black hair.

"Deputy Cal Cooper." He nodded at me, the only one who hadn't met him before. "I understand there's a problem here?"

Cowboy Cal.

He shifted the toothpick in his mouth from one corner to the other and hefted the duffel bag in his hand.

Rose, Wil, and Clara all looked at me.

"There's a body in my room," I said.

The deputy's expression didn't change.

"A dead body," I added. As if we would have called him if it had been any other kind.

"Uh-huh." He looked at the others. "Can any of you corroborate this?"

"Emma told us just a few minutes ago," Rose said. "We thought we should wait until you came before going upstairs."

He leveled his gaze at me and switched the toothpick to the other corner. "Lead the way."

As I opened the door to my suite, Tim meowed from his carrier. At least I had had the presence of mind to put him away until the police could arrive. I led the way around the sectional.

He was still there. Still staring at the ceiling.

Cowboy Cal knelt next to the body and felt for a pulse. "Yup. He's dead." He stood again and stared at the prone figure.

"Who is he?" I asked.

Rose peered at the face. "I know him. It's Dick

Brill, the geologist that I recommended to the Nelsons. They hired him to take them prospecting this week. What is he doing here?"

Everyone looked at me.

"I don't know why he's here," I said, backing away a step. *Dead Dick*, my brain whispered. I shushed it.

"He's in your room," said Wil. "We don't mind if you had a date, but you should have waited until you were off duty."

"It's not like that." I looked at Clara, then at Rose. The frown on her face made my heart sink. The last thing I wanted to do was add more drama to her life. "I've never seen him before, and I don't know how he ended up in my room."

"What do you think, Cal?" Rose asked. "Can you tell how long he's been here?"

Cal took latex gloves from his pocket and pulled them on. He moved the floor lamp nearer to the body, looking at it closely. He grasped the head between his hands and turned it to one side, then the other.

I stopped watching and sat on the couch, suddenly woozy. "Shouldn't he wait for the coroner? That's what they do in all the television shows."

"I'm the deputy coroner," said Cal from behind the couch. "In a county as spread out as ours, the sheriff's department does double duty."

After a couple minutes, the deputy expelled a long sigh, then stood and stripped off his gloves.

"My preliminary report will say he died from a blow to the head, somewhere between twelve and twenty-four hours ago. The coroner will be able to narrow that window once we get him back to the morgue." He put on fresh gloves and got out his camera. He took several pictures of the empty wine bottle. "This could be the murder weapon." He placed it in a plastic bag.

Wil shot a look at me. "Were you drunk, Emma?"

Rose put an arm around my shoulders. "Who could have done it?" she asked.

"Too early to tell." The toothpick switched sides again. "It would help my investigation if Emma would tell us when he got here and what led up to his death."

"An investigation?" Wil asked. "Then you think Emma killed him."

"At this point, everyone is a suspect." He leveled his gaze at me. "Are you going to tell me what happened?"

I crossed my arms. "I told you. I walked into my suite earlier, and there he was."

Cal took out a notepad. "What time was this?"

"About four-fifteen. Our last guests had arrived, and I had shown Mary up to the rooms she and Paul had reserved." I closed my eyes, going through the afternoon in my memory. "She took her luggage in, and then I saw Tim."

"Tim?"

"My cat." I nodded toward the cat carrier just inside the bedroom door. "I don't know how he got into the lounge, but I brought him back in here. That's when I saw the shoes." I pointed to them, still lying on the floor between the big square ottoman and the couch.

"Did you touch the body or move it in any way?"

"No, of course not." I shuddered, then remembered. "Wait, I did touch his shoulder. I thought he was asleep, but he just kind of slumped over onto his back."

"He was lying on his side when you first found him?"

"Yes."

"Mm-hmm." Cal made more notes on his pad and shoved it into his pocket. "I'll call to have the body transported to the coroner's office. Meanwhile, I'd appreciate it if no one mentions this until we can contact the next of kin." He pointed at Wil's cell phone. "Especially on social media. No photos. And we need to seal off the room. No one is allowed in until we clear the scene."

As Cal escorted all of us out of the suite, I grabbed Tim's carrier and litter box and followed behind. Cal stopped me as I went through the doorway.

"I need your key." The deputy held out his hand. I set Tim on the floor, pulled my key from my pocket and dropped it in his latex-gloved palm.

"Until I say otherwise, no one is to enter this room," he said. "And you-" he pointed at me. "I need you to come to the sheriff's office in the morning to give an official statement."

"What about my clothes? And other things? How long do I have to stay out of my room?"

As he closed the door in my face, Cal's last words sounded through it. "I'll let you know."

I stared at the door. There was no way I was going to bullied by some small-town sheriff's deputy. I put my hand on the lever to open it again, but Rose stopped me.

"Come along, dear." She picked up the cat carrier. "You and Tim can stay in my suite tonight. I'm sure everything will be cleared up by morning."

Morning. Our first breakfast. Guests to take care

of. Would any of us get any sleep with Dead Dick on our minds? Would Cowboy Cal be out of our hair before the guests arrived back at the inn this evening?

"Don't worry, Emma," Wil said, walking down the stairs in front of me. "We'll stick by you through the trial. Although I don't know why you thought you needed to kill someone on your second day here."

I was just about to help him down the staircase with a well-planted foot when he turned and grinned at me.

"Come on. It was just a joke."

Rose pushed past him. "Not a very tasteful one, Wil. Emma has had quite a shock, finding poor Dick in her room like that."

Clara patted my shoulder as she followed Rose. "Don't worry. Rose is right. Everything will be cleared up by morning."

Wil went on to the kitchen while Clara, yawning, went to her own room.

"Poor Clara," Rose said, taking Tim's carrier into her spacious suite. "She's still feeling the jet lag from her trip."

I seized the opportunity to talk about anything other than the body in my room.

"She lives in the UK? I thought I heard a Scottish accent."

"That's right. Her home is near Inverness, in the Highlands." She smiled as if the thought brought back delightful memories. "We've known each other since we were young girls, and I cherish her friendship." She set Tim down near a large stone fireplace in the corner of her living room. "I'm sorry, but you'll have to sleep on the couch. I'm using the second bedroom for my office."

"I don't mind at all," I looked around for a good spot for the litter box.

"Put Tim's facilities in the bathroom, and we'll get some of the emergency toiletries from the inn's storeroom for you to use."

Once we had the supplies for me and the extra bag of cat food I had left in the pantry, Rose let Tim out of his carrier and put the tea kettle on her stove to heat up. She pulled a plate of sliced meats and cheeses out of the refrigerator, and we made sandwiches. When the tea was ready, we tucked ourselves into the cozy armchairs that flanked the fireplace. Rose had put another log on the low fire and the heat was enough to chase away the chill I had been feeling ever since discovering Dead Dick in my room.

"Now, Emma," Rose began in a no-nonsense tone, "I want you to tell me the truth. Did you have anything to do with Dick's death?"

"No." I set my cup down on the side table. "I have no idea what happened."

"I didn't think so, but I needed to get that question out of the way." She sipped her tea as if we were discussing the menu for breakfast rather than a murder. "It's important that Cal believes you, too. He's a fair man and a good judge of character."

That's when I saw the line crease her forehead again.

"But you're worried about something."

She shook her head and let a smile smooth away any evidence of her concerns.

"I was only wondering, why you? Why did the murderer hide the body in your suite? You don't have any enemies, do you?"

I smiled back, letting the past stay in the past.

"Not on this continent." I made myself a sandwich with a cracker and a slice of cheese. "What enemies did Dick have?"

"I can't imagine that he had any. He was such a nice man. Everyone liked him."

"Not everyone, it seems."

"I just hope he didn't stumble onto something and was killed for it." Rose finished her tea.

I took a bite of my sandwich. A dead body. A murder investigation. Someone trying to frame me. And I had thought spending the summer in the Black Hills would be a peaceful change from Chicago.

The night had been long and sleepless. Rose's couch had been comfortable enough, but Dead Dick's face swam through my thoughts along with the endless questions of why he was in my room, how he had gotten there, and who knew about it. And every time I flipped over, the digital display on Rose's DVD player reminded me that five o'clock was coming too quickly. Finally, just after I had closed my eyes again, my phone alarm went off.

By the time I had showered, dressed, fed Tim, and looked for Aunt Rose's coffee maker - unsuccessfully - it was time to prepare the dining room for breakfast. I closed Rose's apartment door gently, glancing at the nameplate as the door pressed closed against the padded frame. The name was Evangeline, and a watercolor of a single rose, blush pink with a white center, was below the brass nameplate. I fingered the frame, relishing the beauty and peace of the simple blossom. If only the day ahead would be as calming.

Voices drifted from the direction of the kitchen, and I followed the sound.

"I ordered a dozen blueberry muffins, not an assortment." Wil's voice held an edge to it that he normally reserved for Thatcher.

"You always order an assortment. Gran said you must have made a mistake, and I should bring the usual."

The female voice had a hint of humor in it, as if she wasn't afraid of Wil's artistic whims. I stopped in the doorway. The young woman facing Wil had long black hair swept up in a ponytail. Wil saw me in the doorway and held up a hand.

"Halt. Don't take a step closer. No one comes into my kitchen."

"Wil, come on. It's the inn's kitchen, not yours. Besides, she's here." I indicated the stranger.

He sniffed as the young woman turned to greet me. She grinned as if it wasn't o'dark-thirty on a chilly spring morning.

"Oh, wow, you must be Emma." She stuck out a hand. "Hi. I'm Becky Graves. I deliver the baked goods for the inn every morning." I shook her hand as she kept talking without seeming to take a breath. "Although it seems Wil could bake, you know, with all his chef's credentials, but he says it's beneath him. He's a chef-" she punctuated the word with air quotes - "not a baker. But hey, it's business for our café, so I'm not knocking it. Anyway, I've been wanting to meet you ever since Rose said you were coming. Don't you just love this place?"

"Yes." I jumped in before she could go on. "Wil, do you have any coffee?"

He poured a cup and stuck it in my hand, then pushed Becky and I into the hall without a word. The door swung on its two-way hinges.

I held the cup up to my nose and took a deep breath. Hot. Strong. No sugar. No cream. I closed my eyes. Heaven. My day could start now.

"Cal told me what happened up here last night."

My eyes popped open. "You know Cal?"

"He's my cousin. He came by the café for supper last night and told us what happened." My face must have shown my shock. "Oh, we won't tell anyone else, don't worry."

"So, who knows?"

"Only me, Gran, my sister Josie and her husband, and their kids. And old Sadie, but she doesn't talk to anyone except her cats."

"You're telling me that he told the entire town of Paragon."

She nodded and led the way toward the dining room. "But we won't spread the word, so don't worry. We're as silent as the grave." She grinned. "Grave? Get it? Our last name is Graves."

I groaned at the joke while she made herself a cup of tea at the bar at the end of the dining room and slung her jacket over the back of a chair. I sat down with her, checking my watch. Five-forty-five. I could sit for a few minutes and drink my coffee.

"Have you lived in Paragon long?" I asked. Becky's happy mood was just what I needed after my short night. My mind supplied the mnemonic, Breezy Becky. She was like a spring breeze.

"My great-great-granddaddy started the town back in the late eighteen-hundreds. Of course, it was just his homestead back then, and the gold mine. But our family has been here ever since."

"You said something about a café?"

"Yup. Gran runs the place, and we all help out. I'm the baker. You know, burger buns, muffins, scones, pies. The works. I get the kitchen early, which suits me. And I'm done with my work and out of there before Gran comes in to make breakfast."

The vision of an aproned woman wielding a spatula and frying bacon on a grill made my stomach growl. I sipped my coffee again.

"And Deputy Cal is your cousin?"

"Yeah. My Aunt Jeanne's oldest. She was a widow but got married again and moved to Denver when Cal was about eight years old. He finally came back home once he grew up." Her eyes grew wide. "I just remembered. Cal said you were supposed to come into town to give your statement this morning and he wanted me to make sure you could get there. Do you need a ride? I've got to go in for supplies for the café. Gran did an on-line order at Sam's Club."

I nodded my thanks. I had already returned my rental car.

"Cal's office isn't in Paragon?"

"Nope. It's in Rapid. I can take you, grab the supplies, then pick you up after if you'd like. We can do lunch before we head back home. I know this great place-"

"Rapid?" I was discovering that I needed to just jump in, or Becky's stream of consciousness chatter would never end.

"Rapid City. No one says the whole name when the one will do. I'll pick you up around ten-thirty? After breakfast?"

I thanked her for the offer, and she left as

Montgomery came down the stairs. Right behind him were Annie and Roger.

"I know it's only a little after six," Montgomery said, "but is there tea available?"

"Of course. Hot water is available twenty-four hours a day, and I'm just getting ready to start a pot of coffee if you would rather have that."

Montgomery brewed himself some English Breakfast tea while Annie and Roger headed toward the door.

"We'll be back in time for breakfast," Roger said. He and Annie were both dressed in hiking clothes.

"Don't get lost."

"We'll stick to the roads. We thought we'd go up past the old mine."

"Have fun, and we'll see you at breakfast."

As they left, Montgomery sat at one of the tables while I started setting the buffet with plates, silverware, and napkins. Rose came out of the Evangeline suite with Thatcher running ahead of her toward the door. She waved to us, then took the dog outside.

Montgomery cleared his throat. "She's something, isn't she?"

I glanced at him. He stared at the front door with a bemused expression.

"Do you mean Aunt Rose?"

He nodded and turned back to his tea, stirring a bit of cream into it. "I rarely meet a woman as accomplished and interesting as your aunt."

I smiled. He was obviously smitten with her. "Yes, she is something."

Breakfast went off without a hitch. Wil had made sliced rolled omelets with spinach and mushroom filling topped with a light drizzle of bechamel sauce. Paired with the muffins Becky had brought and fresh fruit, the guests were impressed. The week was starting out well.

Becky showed up at ten-thirty on the dot and Rose pushed me out the door.

"Now, don't let Deputy Cal bully you," she said, holding Thatcher's collar so he wouldn't follow me. "Just tell the truth and let him take his investigation where it leads."

"Even if it leads him the wrong conclusion?"

Rose smiled. "Don't worry. He's a fair man and won't rest until he reaches the right answers. If you didn't have anything to do with Dick's death, he'll soon prove it."

If?

I smiled my goodbye and went out to Becky's car, trying not to let Rose's slip of doubt throw me off. I knew the truth, but could I convince Cal?

The forty-minute drive into Rapid City went quickly with Becky's non-stop commentary on the town of Paragon, the inn, the scenery, and the sights we passed on our way to the county sheriff's office. The weather was sunny and warm, a complete change from when I had arrived in town a couple days ago. Becky pulled into an empty parking space near the front door.

"When you go in, just ask for Cal. I'll be back to pick you up in a half hour or so. We'll have lunch after that, okay?"

"Thanks, Becky. I don't know what I'd do without you."

She beamed. "Don't worry about it. That's what friends are for, right?"

I went up to the door of the office feeling much better than I had for months. Was Becky's offer of friendship that important?

Yes, I told myself. When is the last time you had a friend? A real friend? High school?

I watched Becky's car stop at the corner, then turn right. Knowing I had at least one person on my side made it easier to face Cal.

The deputy at the door buzzed me right through to Cal's office.

"You must have been expecting me," I said, sitting in the brown vinyl upholstered chair across the desk from him.

"Becky texted me with your ETA," he said, sitting behind his desk with the ever-present toothpick firmly in the corner of his mouth. "Can I get you anything? Coffee?"

"No thanks."

"Then we'll get started."

Cal shuffled through some papers on his desk. He found a blank tablet and a pen, then looked at me.

"What time did the victim arrive at your suite?"

"Victim? Then he really was murdered? I hoped it had been an accident."

Leaning his elbows on his desk, Cal looked at me. "Miss Blackwood, this is an interview. I ask the questions and you answer them. Understand?"

"It's Emma." I squirmed in my seat. "Am I a suspect?"

"Like I said last night, everyone is a suspect at this point." He drew a circle on his tablet. "How long have you known the victim?"

"I don't know him. I've never seen him before."

"Then what was he doing in your suite?"

"I don't know." And I wasn't about to begin speculating.

"What time did you leave your room?"

"At seven in the morning."

He wrote the time inside the circle and drew lines across it as if he was cutting a pie. "You didn't return at all during the day?"

"We were busy getting ready for the guests to arrive."

He made a note in another pie shape. "What time did they show up?"

"Clara was the first, and she arrived just after three o'clock. Rose had picked her up at the airport and brought her to the inn."

More notes.

"What time did Rose leave for the airport?"

I thought back. "It was after lunch. Probably around twelve-thirty."

"Who else was at the inn before the guests arrived?"

"Just Wil." I remembered the scones. "And Becky must have come by sometime to deliver the scones for afternoon tea, but I didn't see her."

"When did Mr. Brill show up?"

"I never saw him."

"Right." Cal made another note. "And how much time passed between finding the body and when Wil called?"

"It was at least half an hour. Maybe closer to forty-five minutes. It seemed like it was forever. I waited until all the guests had left for the evening before I told Rose about the man in my room."

Cal bounced his pen again.

I shifted in my seat. "Is there something you

haven't told me?"

"After further examination, the coroner determined that Dick Brill's body was moved post-mortem."

My head swirled. "Moved? You mean more than when he turned from his side to his back?"

"Perhaps someone planted his body in your room to throw suspicion on you." He leaned back in his chair, watching me. "Unless, of course, you're the one who moved him after he died."

"Why would I do that?"

"To cover up the fact that a man died in your suite. Maybe you intended to get rid of the body later."

"But then why would I tell Rose? Why would I have Wil call you?"

He shrugged. "Maybe you got cold feet."

My stomach churned. I began to wish I hadn't eaten a second peach muffin.

Cal leaned on his desk again, his dark brown eyes boring into mine.

"Emma, did you murder Dick Brill?"

Three

"What do you mean, did I murder Dick Brill?" My knees trembled and I was glad I was sitting down. Cal didn't move a muscle. "I found his body, but that was all. I didn't know he was in my suite. I didn't murder him."

My voice was rising even though I tried to keep calm. It was time to shut up. I clamped my mouth closed.

Cal didn't say a thing but kept staring. Waiting for me to talk myself into a confession.

I knew this trick. I had seen it plenty of times on television police dramas. The stare. I could wait as long as any deputy sheriff.

Finally, he sat back in his chair, still staring. "How did he end up in your suite?"

I sighed. He had circled back. "I have no idea." I congratulated myself for keeping my voice even.

"Somebody does."

I leaned forward. "You're right. Somebody does. We just need to find out who."

His eyebrows rose. "Oh, no ma'am. There is no 'we.' You are not going to involve yourself in my investigation, do you understand?"

"What I understand is that I'm already involved.

36

Somebody involved me when they put Dead Dick in my room."

The toothpick twitched. "Dead Dick?"

I put both hands over my mouth. "I can't believe I said that out loud." I lowered my hands. "I'm so sorry. That was inappropriate. In my profession it's important to remember people's names, so I use mnemonics."

"You mean like alliterative nicknames?"

I nodded.

Cal leaned forward. "What is your mnemonic for me?"

My face must have been turning all shades of red. "It doesn't mean anything, you know. It's just a word game."

"Let me see." Cal put his pen down, the interview apparently forgotten. "Cool Cal? Considerate Cal?"

I shook my head. "Cowboy Cal."

He grimaced. "At least it's something I can live with."

"So," I said, rising from my chair, "you have my statement. What's our next step?"

"My next step is to wait for the autopsy results. Your next step is to go home."

"You still think he died from the blow to his head?"

"That was my initial impression, but the coroner has the last word." He ushered me out of his office and down the hall. "I'll let you know if I need anything else from you."

Before we entered the lobby, I paused. "You'll let me know what the coroner says, won't you?"

"Why?"

"Just call it curiosity. I don't like to leave questions

unanswered."

"I'll see you around Paragon." He opened the front door for me. "But I hope I don't get any more calls to show up at the inn."

"I'm sure you won't." I paused on the threshold. "You will tell me what the coroner says, right? Do you have my number?"

"Rose gave it to me. And I'll let you know if I need anything more from you."

"You mean if the report shows something hinky."

The toothpick twitched again. "Hinky?"

"Screwy. Suspicious."

"Right. You'll hear from me in that case."

By the time I reached Becky's SUV, she was grinning like the proverbial Cheshire Cat.

"You and Cal certainly looked chummy," she said as I slid into the passenger seat.

"He turned out to be a pretty nice guy, considering."

"Considering?" She put the car in gear and backed out of the parking space, then drove to the corner stop sign.

"Considering he thinks I murdered Dick Brill."

"Did he say that?"

"I think it was mostly to see my reaction."

Becky drove a few blocks, then parked in front of an ice cream shop.

I looked at the sign. "Armadillos?"

"Just the best ice cream anywhere. And great lunches, too." She stepped out of the car. "Are you coming?"

Becky ordered sandwiches and chips for both of us and led me to a booth, carrying our chips. I followed with our drinks.

"Now, tell me everything," she said. "What did you think of him?"

"Cal? He's a nice guy."

Becky unwrapped a straw and stuck it in her drink. "You know he's single, right?"

"We didn't talk about it." I popped my straw into my drink and took a sip. "Is he single as in never married, or single as in divorced and looking for someone new?"

"Never married." She leaned closer. "Can you believe it? A catch like him getting away?"

I shrugged. "Some people just haven't found the right person."

The girl at the counter called Becky's name and she went to get our sandwiches. I rolled my empty straw wrapper between my fingers, thinking about Cal. Becky was right. From the little I knew about him he would make a great boyfriend for someone. Maybe even a great husband. But who was I to talk? I hadn't found anyone either and time was slipping away.

Becky sat down and handed me a ham and cheese sandwich. A dill pickle spear on the plate made me smile.

"I didn't know places still used these." I took a bite of mine. "I haven't had one in forever."

"Where have you been that you haven't had a dill pickle with your sandwich?"

"Not the States." I finished off my pickle and Becky slid hers onto my plate. I toyed with it as I considered the past two and a half years. "Let's see, the last place was Cancun for eighteen months."

"Rough life." She grinned, then took a bite of her sandwich.

"Before that was St. Kitts." I bit into my sandwich. The roll was delicious, and ham and cheese was my favorite. I opened my bag of green onion chips as I tried to forget the disastrous six months in St. Kitts. "Before that was Norway."

"Not the tropics?"

I shook my head. "Tropical locations are fine, but Norway was very special. The Black Hills reminds me of it in some ways, with the northern climate and the pine trees."

"What took you to those places? Your job?"

"I worked for an international hotel chain. It was exciting to live in all those different locations, and I enjoyed my job. But that's over now." Over and done with. The company had called it "downsizing."

Becky watched me as she chewed the last bite of her sandwich and took a long drink.

Finally, she leaned on the table. "It might have been exciting, but I think I would hate it. All that time without a real home? No family around? Not for me."

I poked at the last few crumbs of my chips. "It did get a little lonely at times. Maybe that's why I'm glad Rose invited me to work at the inn this summer. She's the only family I have and I'm happy to get the opportunity to know her better."

"That's another reason to grab Cal." Becky pointed her last chip at me. "You need a big family around you, and Cal comes with one ready-made. Gran and the cousins will make sure you always have someone to count on." She popped the chip in her mouth. "Let's order our ice cream before the afternoon crowd arrives. The students from the university swamp this place on nice days."

I ordered a sundae called "The Salty Dog" while

Becky asked for an "Armadillo." We took the sundaes to the outside eating area since the inside dining was getting crowded.

"This looks like a popular place," I said, savoring my first bite of ice cream, hot fudge, marshmallow cream, and salted peanuts.

"You should see it on a summer night. The lines go out to the street." Becky scooped up a bite of her ice cream. "Back to Cal-"

I laughed. "You don't give up, do you?"

She lifted her spoon in the air as if she was taking a vow. "Never."

"I promise. I'll give Cal a chance. But you have to let anything between the two of us be his idea. No pushing."

"Hey, as long as you keep an open mind about him, I'm good."

I took another bite of my ice cream and watched as the line at the outside order window grew longer. A young couple set their drinks down on the table near the bench where Becky and I were sitting.

"Emma? What are you staring at?"

"Sorry." I focused on Becky again. "I was just thinking about, um, you-know-who and the situation. Those cups reminded of the wine glasses in my suite."

"Wine glasses?" Becky scooped another bite of ice cream with her spoon. "Sounds very romantic and cozy."

"Oh, come on. I'm trying to be serious."

"Okay. Why wine glasses?"

"Maybe to make it look like he came to my room for a romantic fling? That's the first thing Wil said." I spooned up a glob of marshmallow cream. "But why were there two wine glasses? And an empty wine bottle? That just doesn't make sense."

Becky scraped her spoon on the bottom of her sundae cup. "Not if you were trying to frame someone."

I stuck my spoon in my ice cream and pushed it away. Becky had just echoed the same suggestion Rose had made, and the thought ruined my appetite. "Who would want to frame me?"

"It doesn't have to be you. Just someone, and you were handy."

"But why? And who had an opportunity?"

"You found him during the afternoon tea, right? Who wasn't in the dining room with everyone else?"

I thought back. I had been so flustered about finding Dead Dick that I hadn't noticed much else.

Finally, I shook my head. "I can't remember right now."

"Maybe it will come to you." Becky stood and tossed her cup into a nearby trash can. "Are you ready to go? I need to get Gran's groceries home."

"I need to get back, too. It's almost time to set up for this afternoon's tea."

"That will be the perfect time to review what happened yesterday," Becky said as she beeped the lock on the SUV. "That's when you'll remember who wasn't there and you'll have your man."

"Or woman." I grinned at her.

Who were we kidding? Somehow Dick Brill had hit his head on something, died, and ended up in my room. There was no foul play and no murder. It was probably all just a mistake. Dick had just wandered into the wrong room.

Or I'd wake up tomorrow and find that this had all been just a bad dream.

"The coroner says it was murder, just like I thought."

My phone had rung just as I put the last tray of scones on the buffet, completing the preparations for afternoon tea.

"Cal?"

"Yes, ma'am. I still need you to stay out of your suite for the next few days so we can process the scene completely."

"Can I go in to get my clothes and other things?"

"Wait until I get there. I'll need to make sure you don't contaminate the crime scene."

I chewed my bottom lip. "Um, the crime scene? You think Dick was murdered in my suite?"

"I'll be there in an hour."

I shoved my phone in my back pocket and went around the dining room straightening the chairs. Becky had had a good idea when she suggested I figure out who wasn't present yesterday afternoon. I mentally placed the guests in their chairs as I touched each one. Nora and Sam had sat at this table, and Clara, Rose, and Montgomery had sat at the one to their right. Going around the room counterclockwise, I placed Annie and Roger at the next table. Paul and Mary had come in last. Paul had been holding court while I took Mary upstairs just before I found Dead Dick.

Sighing, I leaned against the buffet counter. Everyone had been present during the afternoon, so it looked like the culprit couldn't be a guest. I reached behind the counter and grabbed my bottle of water.

As I flipped open the top, I thought through the timing. What if Dick had been put in my room before the guests started arriving? I hadn't been in there all day, so it could have happened any time after I had left it in the morning.

I took a drink of water. No. I shook my head. I had been upstairs before lunchtime, and I would have seen Tim in the lounge. So, Dick had to have been put in my room between eleven o'clock and four-thirty.

My mind was still sorting through the problem when Rose came out of her suite.

"Is everything ready for this afternoon's tea?" she asked.

"All we need are the guests." I brought her a cup of her favorite tea as she sat at a table. "Have you made much progress on your memoirs?"

"Not really. Dick's death was such a shock."

"Did you know him well?" I asked as I sat down. It felt good to be off my feet for a few minutes.

Rose stirred a teaspoon of sugar into her tea. "I had attended some of his community education lectures and we were both part of the Conserve the Black Hills initiative."

"What's that?"

"A group of us joined together to keep track of new business ventures in the Black Hills area, especially industrial."

"You mean like logging or mining?"

"Yes." She sipped her tea. "It isn't that we're against those industries, but we want to make sure the companies are concerned with conserving the resources of the area rather than exploiting them. There are several companies that have brought jobs and economic growth to the Black Hills, but still maintain the integrity of the forest."

"Is that why you oppose uranium mining?"

Her eyes flashed as she looked at me. "It's one of the worst types of mining for this area. There is uranium in the Black Hills, but most of it is in such low concentrations that mining it isn't feasible. A lot of expense and trouble for very little gain. However, there are always unscrupulous companies who are willing to cut corners on safety measures to hold their costs down. Dick was our organization's expert, and we relied heavily on his expertise in the fight to protect the forests from those types of mining companies."

I filed that information away. Could it be that one of those unscrupulous companies had resented Dick's opposition?

"You said Sam and Nora had hired Dick?"

"Yes, for one of his gold expeditions, as he called them. He enjoyed teaching whether the university was in session or not. He had a passion for sharing his love of geology with others, especially tourists, which is why he conducted those gold hunting trips. I had recommended him to Sam and Nora since they inquired about doing some prospecting when they made their reservations."

Seeker Sam. If Sam and Nora had met with Dick before they checked into the inn, they could have had a quarrel that ended badly. I couldn't picture Sam or Nora killing anyone, but I didn't know them. Can anyone tell if someone is a murderer at first glance?

I finished my water. "Deputy Cal called a few minutes ago. He'll be over soon to secure the crime scene. I hope he doesn't disturb your writing. I can't wait to read your memoirs."

It might have been nosy on my part, but I was curious about Rose's life. My father had never wanted to talk about his brother Harry, Rose's husband. Harry had died in an accident when I was a young girl and my father had not spoken to Rose since then. Because of that, Rose's life had always been a mystery to me. I knew she was often out of the country for her work, but when she retired a few years ago, she had opened the inn. In our emails and phone calls, she only chatted about the present, not the past. All I knew was that Dad blamed her for Harry's death, but I couldn't imagine why.

Rose shook her head. "No one will read them until after I'm gone." She squeezed my hand as the front door opened. "Our guests are returning from their excursions." Her blue eyes twinkled. "I love to hear what they've been up to all day. I'll act as hostess for the tea so you can take care of Cal when he comes."

"You don't mind?"

"Not at all. This is my favorite part of being an innkeeper."

I made my way to the reception desk to intercept Cal when he arrived and met Annie and Roger as they entered, sunburned from their day of hiking. They said a quick hello, then went upstairs. Montgomery was right behind them.

"Rose, you were right." His boisterous baritone carried throughout the inn. "That museum had just the information I needed."

He made a cup of tea and sat down at Rose's table.

"Will you go back, or did you find everything?"

"I need to spend more time delving into mining records, but not tomorrow. I'd like to go up to the mine. You say it's safe?"

"Safe enough. There was a cave-in years ago that blocked access to the deeper shafts, so it is easy to find your way in and out without getting lost."

Clara was next to arrive with Cowboy Cal right behind her. I clasped my hands together to control their nervous shaking. I had no reason to be worried about what Cal might find in my suite. Clara joined Rose and Montgomery, but Cal planted himself at the bottom of the stairway. He switched the toothpick from one side of his mouth to the other.

"You haven't gone into your rooms for any reason, have you?"

After the friendly way our interview had ended that morning, I had thought Cal might have eased up on his professional bluntness, but he was as stiff as ever.

"Of course not."

Cal leaned on the reception desk, his steady gaze pinning me in place. "Why not?"

"You told me not to."

The toothpick switched sides and the corners of his eyes crinkled. "I hoped you'd be the 'follow the rules' type."

Was he flirting with me? In spite of the crinkles, no smile appeared. I glanced toward the dining room. The afternoon tea was in Rose's capable hands, and she had Wil to help if she needed him. I led the way up to my suite and waited while Cal unlocked the door.

Cal set his duffel bag on the floor, removed some paper foot coverings, and handed me a pair.

I held them up. "Really? After we were all in my suite last night?"

"Standard procedure." Cal grabbed a roll of yellow tape from his duffel and started unrolling an end.

"Um, I know that's standard procedure, too," I said as I balanced on one foot to slip the footie over my shoe. "But do you have to put it over the doorway? We don't want the guests to get the wrong idea."

The toothpick switched sides again. "Don't you think they already know about it?"

He handed me a pair of disposable gloves and snapped his own pair over his hands.

On the other side of the stairway, the Westerland room's door opened, and Annie and Roger appeared. They stared, comprehension moving swiftly across their faces. Then they grinned at each other, and Roger hurried toward us.

"Is this where it happened?" he asked, trying to peer into my room as Cal pulled the door closed.

Annie lagged behind him. "Have you seen..." Her voice dropped. "...his ghost?"

Roger grabbed his wife's arms. "Wouldn't it be great if Paul could film his show right here? The episode could be called, 'The Ghost of Sweetbrier Inn.'"

"There are no ghosts," I said, "and no television shows are going to be filmed in my suite."

"That's what they all say," Roger said, "then one night you'll hear a ghostly noise or see a shadowy figure and then you'll call Paul in to chase the ghost for you."

Cal waited until the pair were on their way down the stairs before he opened the door again. I heard Roger say something about setting up surveillance outside my room that night.

"I wish they wouldn't do that." I followed Cal into my living room.

"What? Keep a lookout for non-existent ghosts? They don't mean any harm. Most people don't know how to react when they come face to face with death, or even brush shoulders with it. Their plans are harmless." Cal pushed my bedroom door open. "I have to take a look in here before you go in."

"What do you expect to find?"

"I hope there will be nothing. But I need to check just the same."

"Do you think Dick could have been in my bedroom?"

He didn't answer. I heard him opening the dresser drawers and I peered through the doorway. My bed was still neatly made, and the closet door was closed.

I took a step into the room. "Do you want some help? If there's anything out of place, I'd know."

He looked at me from the other side of the bed where he was crouched on his hands and knees looking underneath it. "You mean you'd know if anything was missing?"

"Or moved."

"Or moved." His face showed disbelief. He got up and motioned me in. "Okay. Take a look at the bathroom. What do you think?"

I stood in the bathroom doorway. The shower door was open slightly, with the bathmat hung over the top to dry. My toothbrush was in its holder, the soap in its dish, and the washcloth hung from the towel rack next to the hand towel. The stack of extra towels in the cubby under the sink was three high, just as I had left them.

"Everything is in order."

Cal's eyebrows raised. "You left your room this clean, and you weren't expecting company?"

I crossed my arms. "I know. I'm a little OCD. I like things to be orderly."

"Okay, then. Pack what you need for the next few days. I'll start in the living room."

"Dusting for prints?"

He switched his toothpick again. "You watch too many detective shows."

I got my suitcase out of the closet and opened the dresser drawers. Knit slacks, tee shirts, and cardigans. I was used to packing and moving, and my clothes were minimal. Life was just easier that way

Cal called from the living room. "Can you come in here for a minute?"

He crouched by the sofa. The wine glasses were still on the tray, but he had moved the ottoman, and underneath, next to where one of Dead Dick's shoes had been, was a flake of something greenish gray, about an inch across.

"Is that a leaf?" I leaned closer to it.

"It's lichen. It grows everywhere in the Hills. You find it on rocks, mostly."

"What is it doing here?"

"Have you been up in the hills at all? Hiking around Rose's property, or walking up the road?"

"Only when I took Thatcher out for his walk yesterday afternoon. But I went down toward Paragon, not up the hill."

"Could this be from your shoe?"

I shook my head. "I changed my shoes in the garage."

Cal took a numbered plastic tab out of his duffel bag, put it next to the lichen, then snapped a photo.

Excitement bubbled up. "Just like on television!"

Picking up the lichen with a pair of tweezers, Cal dropped it into a small bag and sealed it. "Sometimes they do things right on those shows." He wasn't smiling.

"You still think I had something to do with Dick's death?"

"I told you, at this point-"

"Everyone is a suspect." I returned his stony stare. "I know. But I also know the truth. I wasn't in my room all day. I didn't have anything to do with his body being here."

The toothpick switched sides, then he looked around the room. "Are you ready to go?"

"I need to finish packing."

I went back into the bedroom. Cal watched me as I loaded the rest of my clothes into the suitcase.

"You travel light," he said.

"That's because I travel a lot." I zipped the suitcase closed. "Or I used to. Old habits, you know."

He walked with me to the door. "Tomorrow is Sunday and my day off. By Monday we should have the complete coroner's report, not just the preliminaries."

"Do you think more details will show up that will get me off the hook?"

"Or more details that incriminate you." The stony look was back. "Make sure you stay out of this room until I give you clearance to use it again."

I left Cal to finish whatever investigating he wanted to do and headed down to Rose's suite. The deputy had to find fingerprints or something. Anything to clear my name off the suspect list.

Four

After breakfast the next morning, I went to church with Rose and Clara. The small white building was quaint and peaceful, sitting at the edge of Paragon with its back to the creek. A cemetery had been placed on a high spot next to the church. As we walked by, I saw that the place was filled with Graves. Most of the markers bore that family name.

Before church started, I met Becky's Gran, her great-aunt Sophie, and so many aunts, uncles, and cousins that I couldn't keep track of the names. Cal sat in the center of one pew, flanked on both sides by pre-teen boys.

"Cal must be a favorite," I said to Becky as I waved to him across the sanctuary.

"The boys love him." Becky led the way to a pew, then scooted along it to make room for Rose and me. "He takes them fishing and camping in the forest, both the youngsters and their dads. It's a big family thing for them, but he's the one who organizes the outings and gets everyone on board."

"A real Boy Scout?" I tried to make a joke, but Becky was serious.

"An Eagle Scout," she said. "He does it to keep the traditions of our ancestors alive."

"Ancestors?"

"Lakota. Our family is a blend of Irish and Lakota, thanks to our great-great-grandparents. Many of the in-laws are full Lakota, which makes us all more Lakota than Irish." She grinned. "Gran says we carry the best genes of the world in our family."

The morning passed quickly, but even with the reverent church service and the company of Becky and her family, I couldn't shake the memory of the sight of Dead Dick behind my couch.

I had lunch at the Gran's Café with Rose and Clara, then we walked back to the inn. As we turned off the pavement onto the gravel of Graves' Gulch Road, sunlight made the forest glow with the promise of the summer to come, and the first blues of spring wildflowers dotted the pine needle covered ground.

Rose continued up the driveway to the inn, taking the slope easily, but Clara and I puffed to keep up with her.

"You'll soon get used to the higher altitude," Rose said as she stopped to wait for us. "Why don't we sit on the porch for a while? We have time before the guests arrive home."

Clara waved a hand in surrender. "You two enjoy yourselves. I'm ready for a nap."

"An afternoon nap sounds wonderful," Rose said.

"It's a habit I have no desire to give up," Clara said. "It's the way to stay young." She winked at Rose and went inside.

Rose settled easily into one of the porch chairs and I took the other. The scene of the village below and the mountains on the other side of Paragon's valley was just as lovely as it had been when I first saw it. Closer to us, a rock garden just coming to life filled the slope between the inn and the road. Here and there I saw the barest hint of green spikes growing through the winter's covering of pine needles.

"I don't think I would ever get tired of this view." I leaned back against the soft cushions.

"It is lovely, isn't it?"

The afternoon air was warm and quiet.

"Why did you start the inn?" I asked.

"When I retired five years ago, I didn't want to hide away in some retirement village. I've always wanted to run a B&B, and this was my chance." Rose smiled at the memory.

"Where does Wil fit in? He's your partner, isn't he?"

"My vision for the inn meant that I needed to find a first-class chef. I wanted someone who shared my vision, and I wanted him to commit to it financially as well as with his talents."

I nodded my understanding. "You wanted him to have some skin in the game."

"We're partners. If the inn does well, we both benefit. If we have a poor year, we both take the losses."

"Are you equal partners?"

Rose shook her head. "I'm the senior, owning seventy percent of the business. That percentage gives me control over what happens to the property, but it also gives Wil a large interest in it. It has worked out well for both of us, I think."

"Wil seems to be the first-class chef you were looking for."

"Oh, yes. He invested in the business early on and

helped design the inn. The kitchen is his baby."

"I know! He is like a king lording over his domain in there."

Rose laughed at my description. "It was his idea to build the greenhouse off the garage. Have you seen it?"

"Only a glimpse. What do you grow in there?"

"Wil uses about half of the space for his vegetables. The greenhouse gives him the fresh vegetables and fruits he needs all through the season. The rest of the greenhouse is mine. One of my hobbies is growing herbs and plants to make tea blends. I love dabbling with the different flavors."

A car turned onto Graves' Gulch Road. I recognized Paul Peterson's rented Jeep.

"It looks like our guests are coming home."

Rose looked at her watch. "And just in time for tea." We both rose from our seats. "They all know about the murder, don't they?"

"You know how news like that gets around. Roger and Annie wanted to stake out my room."

"Why?"

"To catch Dick's ghost."

She laughed as she opened the inn's front door. "Maybe Paul could turn the incident into one of his television shows."

"That's what Roger said. I wasn't sure you wanted that kind of publicity."

Rose paused before going into her suite. "Didn't you know? Every inn should have a ghost story."

As she went to take Thatcher on his walk, I cleared away the last few dishes from the morning's breakfast. Wil had Sunday afternoon off, but he had prepared tea sandwiches and put them in the refrigerator for me to serve in the afternoon.

I walked into the kitchen. It was so quiet and empty without Wil there that I felt like I was an intruder.

I opened the refrigerator to get the tray of sandwiches, and as I set them on the prep table in the center of the kitchen, I heard loud voices from the entryway.

"What do I care?" Paul said, his voice bellowing.

"Shh," Mary said. "Someone is going to hear you."

"No one else is here. You saw Rose taking her dog out, and the parking lot is empty."

Silence. I should have let them know I was in the kitchen, but then I heard a soft giggle.

"There, isn't that better?"

Paul's voice held a tone I had never heard from him before. Pleading. Intimate. I couldn't very well step into the middle of whatever they were doing now. I peeked around the corner. Paul and Mary were standing close, his forehead against hers.

"But Paul-"

He pushed her away and stalked three steps toward the kitchen. I jumped back before he could see me.

"Oh, grow up, Mary. What are you afraid of? That your husband will find out about us?"

I peered around the corner again. Mary looked like she was about to cry.

"Look. Do you want this job or don't you?"

Mary blinked fast. "Of course, I do. I don't know what I would do if I couldn't be with you."

Paul strode toward her and took her in his arms. "Come on, baby. Let's go upstairs. Let me show you how much you mean to me."

I was liking Paul less every minute.

As their footsteps faded away, I turned back to the tray of sandwiches and pulled the plastic wrap off.

I had just placed the tray on the buffet when Sam and Nora came in the front door.

"How was your day of sight-seeing?" I asked.

"It was wonderful," Nora said. She walked over to the buffet, took one look at the sandwiches and picked up a plate and napkin. "We went for a walk this morning, then drove up to Deadwood and spent the afternoon browsing through the shops."

Sam took another plate while I started a fresh pot of coffee.

"Nora browsed through the shops," he said, choosing a ham salad sandwich. "I checked out the casinos."

"Any luck?"

He shook his head and picked out a second sandwich, egg salad this time. "This whole vacation is a string of bad luck. First our guide is murdered, and then the craps table took me for a ride."

"Now Sam, you know you always lose at the casinos, no matter which game you play." Nora set her plate on one of the tables and then poured herself a glass of iced tea. "I had a wonderful time, though. I found a new pair of earrings." She pulled her permed curls back and shook her head, making the shiny baubles dance. "Black Hills gold. It might be the only gold I take home."

Rose had come in while we were talking and sat at the round table across from Nora. "Will you be looking for a new guide?"

Nora glanced at Sam as she tore open a blue package and poured the sweetener into her tea.

"I found some leads online," Sam said. He sat in the third chair at the table. "But I'm sure they're all booked up." He shrugged as if it didn't matter. "I'll do my gold-hunting at the casinos."

"If you'd like to learn how to pan for gold, there's a mine in Keystone that gives tours," Rose said. "At the end of the tour, they have a place you can try your hand at panning. They guarantee you'll find gold."

"That sounds like fun," Nora said. "What do you think, sweetie?"

Sam ate his first sandwich in one bite. "Whatever you want, dear." His voice was muffled as he chewed and talked at the same time.

"Then we'll do that tomorrow." Nora gave Rose a bright smile. "Even though our plans were spoiled, we can still have a fun vacation." Her lower lip stuck out in a mock pout. "It's too bad that Dick fellow had to go and get himself killed. Do they have any idea who did it?"

I went into the kitchen to get another pitcher of iced tea. Nora couldn't be as cold as she sounded, could she? I took a scoop of ice from the machine next to the cooler and poured it into the pitcher as I watched Nora chatting with Rose. Or was she a brilliant foil to Sam's murderous schemes? He had just shoved his second sandwich in his mouth and was chewing with a frown on his face, paying no attention to his wife.

At this point, I could see the two of them plotting to kill Dick.

But that was just my imagination trying to find a new suspect for Cal - any suspect other than the only one he had so far.

Besides, what would be their reason for killing

Dick? Without him to guide them on their gold hunt, Nora was right. All their plans were ruined.

On Monday morning I snagged my first cup of coffee from Wil before I started setting up for breakfast. He was making goat cheese and spinach quiches in individual ramekins, and they smelled delicious.

"Becky hasn't delivered the pastries yet?" I sipped my coffee. Wil knew how to brew the stuff. I savored the rich dark roast.

"Not yet," he said, taking a tray of six quiches from the oven. He set them on the stainless-steel counter and peered across their tops.

I leaned on my elbows, trying to see what he was seeing.

"What are you doing?" He frowned at me.

"I'm trying to figure out what you're doing."

"If you must know, I'm making sure they're done."

"Aren't you supposed to stick a toothpick in them or something?"

He snorted as he started breaking eggs into a mixing bowl. "That's what happens in your grandmother's kitchen. Most chefs use a quick-read thermometer, but I don't want to spoil the surface of the quiches."

"So how do you know if they're done?"

"That's my secret."

Wil turned his back to me, hiding whatever ingredients he was putting into the quiche mixture.

Fine. If he wanted to act like the stereotypical chef, let him. I sniffed the savory aroma again. I could put up with anything as long as he produced breakfasts like this.

"Hey guys." Becky breezed into the kitchen carrying a stack of pastry boxes. "Sorry I'm running late. The old oven wasn't cooperating again today. I keep telling Gran we need to buy a new one, but she refuses."

She set the boxes down on the end of the counter and waved the invoice toward Wil for his signature.

He gave her one glance, then nodded at me. "Emma can sign it. I'm busy."

Becky rolled her eyes as she gave me the invoice. "Mister I-can't-be-bothered-with-the-small-stuff is in charge again, I see."

I skimmed the bill. "Ooh, raspberry and cream cheese croissants?"

"I thought you'd like those instead of the usual blueberry or banana muffins for breakfast. I got a deal on the raspberries and had to use them up." She picked up the stack of boxes again. "Wil, do you want me to put these in the cooler?"

"Yeah, sure." He didn't pause as he poured the filling into waiting ramekins for the next batch of quiches.

"Let me help you carry those," I said, taking the top two boxes from the stack.

Becky balanced her three boxes on one arm and pulled the cooler door open.

"Hey," Wil said. "If you two ladies are done putting the groceries away, get out of here. I'm trying to work."

Becky met Wil's rudeness with her signature

'whatever' look. "I've got to get back to the café anyway. If that old oven goes out again, Gran will need me."

I walked down the hall to the garage with her, and when we opened the door, Becky stifled a scream. I swung the door open the rest of the way. Paul Peterson was standing at the bottom of a flight of stairs that ran up the back wall of the garage, his hand on the rail.

He ran the other hand through his wavy blond hair. "Hi."

"Hi, Paul." I took a step inside the garage with Becky behind me. "Can I help you find something?"

He looked up the flight of stairs, then around the garage. When his gaze reached the side door at the far end of the garage that led to the parking lot, he pointed at it.

"There it is," he said, taking a few steps in that direction, "I needed to get something from the car and thought the door by the kitchen led to the parking lot." He chuckled. "I didn't realize I'd end up in here."

I put on my professional face, the one that took no nonsense from guests. "The garage is for the staff only. We would appreciate it if you used the front door."

"Oh, sure." He didn't even blush. "I'll just go this way now, as long as I'm here, but I'll remember to use the main door from now on."

He waved as he left, shutting the door firmly behind him.

"What was that all about?" Becky asked.

"I don't know." I walked over to the steps. "Do you know where this staircase leads?"

"To Wil's apartment. He lives over the garage, you know."

"But I thought the door to his place is upstairs, down the hall past the Westerland."

"Yes, there are two doors. This way he has a private entrance and can come and go without bothering the guests."

We went out the front entrance next to the big garage doors and walked toward Becky's SUV.

"Are you still worried about Dick's death?"

"Does it show?" I tried to smile. "It doesn't help that I'm the prime suspect."

"Cal isn't going to arrest you. He doesn't have any evidence, does he?" She gave me a doubtful look. "Unless he does. You aren't a murderer, are you?"

"Oh, not you, too!"

Becky laughed. "I'll see you later."

Annie and Roger were the first ones down for breakfast. Wil's quiche and fruit salad paired with Becky's croissants made Annie moan with delight.

"This is so good," she said. "My compliments to the chef."

I looked across the buffet and into the kitchen. Wil gave me a smug look and a slight bending at the waist that seemed more like an acknowledgment of a deserved ovation than a bow.

"He heard you and appreciates the compliment," I said as I refilled the couple's coffee cups. "What do you two have planned for today?"

Roger stirred cream into his coffee. "We had hoped Paul would invite us to come along on his ghost hunting trip into the mine, but he hasn't said anything about it. So, we thought we'd hike up to Black Elk Peak. Do you know anything about the trail?"

I shook my head, making a mental note to learn more about the area. "I'm new here and haven't had a chance to explore yet."

"We'll let you know what it's like, then. We met some hikers yesterday afternoon who said there was still a lot of snow up near the fire tower. In April! Can you imagine?"

Annie picked through her fruit salad. She seemed to be waiting for something.

"I hope you have a good hike," I said.

Sam and Nora came downstairs talking loudly.

"I don't care if you do want to try another casino, I want to go someplace else," Nora said. "I have more shopping to do."

Sam dropped his voice. "You know I have work to do."

"So, drop me off in town. I'll find someone else to go shopping with." Nora's face brightened when she saw Annie. "How about you, dear? Do you want to go to Rapid City with me today?"

Annie pushed her breakfast dish away. "Sorry, no. Roger and I have plans."

"More hiking?" Nora helped herself to a quiche and two croissants. "I don't know how you do it." She licked some cream cheese off her finger and laughed. "I don't even know why you do it."

Roger stood and held his hand out to Annie. "The views are stupendous. You should try it."

Nora waved them away with one hand while she set her plate on an empty table. "I don't think so. But you two have fun."

Roger and Annie went upstairs to their room, passing Montgomery on his way down.

"Good morning, all," he said. He made himself a cup of tea and set it on the table next to Sam and Nora's. "Did I hear you say you were going to Rapid City today?" he asked Sam.

"Yeah." Sam shoved a bite of quiche into his mouth.

"Then you won't be going back to the mine?"

Sam shot him a look. "Who says I was at the mine?"

"I thought I saw you there yesterday."

Montgomery looked calm and relaxed as he chose a quiche and a croissant, but Sam's face was red.

"Some people need to mind their own business," he said, glaring at Montgomery's back. "We were in Deadwood yesterday."

"No matter. My mistake." Montgomery looked up as the door to Rose's suite opened. "Ah, here's the fair flower. Come have breakfast with me, Rose."

She smiled at him and tugged her sweater on. "As soon as I take Thatcher for his morning walk." She had him on his leash already. "I'll be back in half an hour or so."

I looked at Montgomery, expecting to see the look of a smitten man, but instead his eyes were narrowed as he watched Rose leave. Not smitten. Thoughtful.

My phone rang. Cal's name was on the screen, so I stepped into the hall to answer it.

"Hey, what's up?"

"Is that how you always answer the phone?"

"When it's someone I know. When can I move back into my suite?"

He paused. I imagined the toothpick tilting as he chewed on it.

"I thought I'd stop by the inn before I go into the

office this morning. The head coroner emailed his final report last night."

"If you get here in time, you could have breakfast."

He paused again. "Um, well, Gran already fed me."

"Let me guess. Scrambled eggs, pancakes, sausage, and hash browns?"

He actually chuckled. "You know Gran."

"You could have had quiche."

The snort on the other end of the line could have been laughter. "I'll be over in a few minutes."

Three minutes on the dot. Roger and Annie had left for their hike, Sam and Nora had gone back to their room, and Clara was keeping Montgomery company while he waited for Rose to return from her walk. I hadn't heard a peep from Mary, and I hadn't seen Paul come back into the building yet. I hoped he hadn't decided to come back through the garage when he thought he wouldn't be caught.

Cal pulled off his reflective sunglasses as he strode in the door. I had to admit that his sheepskin jacket and cowboy hat were ruggedly appealing.

"Is there somewhere we can talk?"

Down to business, as usual. I glanced into the dining room. Montgomery and Clara were chatting over their cups of tea and wouldn't miss me.

"Let's step into Rose's suite. She's out walking Thatcher."

Tim greeted me at the door, and I scooped him up. With Thatcher around, Tim hadn't gotten much attention lately. I scratched the white spot on his chest.

"This is like an apartment," Cal said, looking

around the living room. "Nice fireplace."

The stone fireplace that filled the corner of the room with its exposed stone chimney had drawn me the first time I had seen it, too.

I sat on the couch. "Rose has lovely taste, doesn't she?"

"One bedroom, living room, kitchen?"

"And an office." I pointed toward the door Rose always kept locked. "The suite is a good size for one person, but it's a little cramped right now."

"I get your point." Cal opened the file he had carried in. "I have the coroner's report here. There's one thing missing."

"What?"

"The murder weapon. We didn't find it in your suite."

"Wasn't it the wine bottle? That's what you thought the other night."

"It was something else."

Cal was being infuriatingly vague.

"If you can't find the murder weapon, you know that Dick couldn't have been killed there."

He raised his eyebrows. "Not necessarily. You could have gotten rid of it after you killed him."

I stared at him. "Do you think I would get rid of the weapon but leave the body behind?" He shifted his gaze away from me. "What did kill him?"

"A rock. Rose quartz, specifically."

"You can tell what kind of rock it was?"

"There were bits of it embedded in the wound." Cal held up a photo. "If you look closely, you can see them."

I didn't move closer. "I'll take your word for it." I chewed my bottom lip, then stopped. I needed to break that habit. "You know that all the evidence you have against me is circumstantial, right?"

"Right. It also doesn't add up. I can't construct a reasonable timeline from the evidence I have, which makes me think you were right about someone framing you. And that is why I'm taking you off the suspect list. I wouldn't share this information with you otherwise."

A light glimmered in my mind. "You're saying I can help you solve the case?" Tim jumped to the floor as I shifted forward in my seat. "You need my help, don't you?"

"Becky said you were looking for leads on your own. I'd rather keep an eye on what you're doing."

"So, you'll share your evidence with me?"

"Not all of it. But if you keep me in the loop, we can work together up to a point. You have to promise to keep things confidential, though."

I leaned against the back of the couch, "Up to a point? Which point is that? The one where I feed you all the information and you solve the case while I hide in the background?"

Cal closed the file and tapped one finger on it while he stared at me. Rose's grandfather clock chimed the quarter hour.

"Hiding in the background is a good idea," he finally said. He leaned forward, dangling the folder in his hands. "There is a murderer out there, and he or she might be willing to kill again. Investigating this case could be dangerous, and the risk will be greater the closer we get to the solution."

I grinned.

Cal frowned. "What?"

"You said 'we.'" I did a fist pump. "I'm working

the case with you."

"Didn't you hear the part about it being dangerous?"

"Of course, I did. But the faster we solve the case, the less likely it is that anyone else gets hurt."

Cal stood. "As long as that anyone else isn't you."

I studied his face. The frown was still there, but there was something else in his eyes. "You're worried about me?"

He shoved his sunglasses back on and started for the door.

"Just keep in touch. Report anything to me that you think might have a bearing on the case." He paused with his hand on the doorknob. "Anything. Got that?"

I nodded as he opened the door and we stepped into the foyer. "Anything."

"You can move back into your room. I've cleared it."

"Thank you." I crossed my arms. "And what's our next move?"

"Keep your eyes and ears open." Cal looked past me into the dining room where Montgomery and Clara were still talking. No one else was in sight. "The murderer is probably connected with the inn, and possibly with you."

"But I just got here a few days ago. No one knows me around here."

He put his hat on. "Keep open to any possibility. Someone could have followed you here, or perhaps the guy chose your room at random. Maybe your door was unlocked, which gave him an opportunity."

Door unlocked...

"I just thought of something." I scrunched my

eyes closed, thinking back. "When I went to put Tim back in my room after I found him in the upstairs lounge on Friday afternoon, I had to unlock my door to get in."

"Are you sure?"

I opened my eyes. "I'm sure. I remember putting the key in the lock, and I remember hearing the latch open when I turned the key. Whoever put Dick's body into my room had a key."

Cal's radio beeped and he pulled from his belt and glanced at the screen. "I've got to get to the office." He shoved it back into his belt. "You have your first assignment then. Figure out who had access to your room. Track down all the keys and where they're kept." He turned toward the front door, talking as he went. "Got that?"

"Yes, sir." I gave him a mock salute.

"And Emma," he said, opening the door, "take this seriously, okay?"

"Don't worry." I swallowed, trying to settle my nervous stomach. "I will."

Five

I considered Cal's warning as I started my morning work of tidying up the guest rooms. Thinking that I might be the target of a murderer was not pleasant, so instead I focused on who could have had access to my room.

Rose used an old-fashioned key system for the inn. Every door had a retro-looking key attached to a metal key ring with the inn's logo and address on it. They were bulky so they didn't get lost easily, but they were also compact enough to fit in a pocket or a purse. There were three keys for each room. Each of the occupants were given one when they checked in and the spare keys were kept in a locked box at the reception desk. As I went over the system again in my mind, I had to admit that it was secure enough for an inn the size of the Sweetbrier.

In Annie and Roger's room, the Westerland, I exchanged the fresh towels I had brought in for the soiled ones, then made the bed. These routine chores were done by the housekeeping staff in the other hotels where I had worked, but here at the inn they were my responsibility. I restocked the tissues and toilet paper and placed two mints on the pillow shams. Gathering the used towels under one arm, I closed and locked the door.

Stopping, I stared at the key in my hand. The murderer hadn't needed the key to my room. He could have used a master key, like I had just done. How many master keys were there? I made a mental note to ask Rose and went on to the rest of the rooms.

After I finished, I carried the soiled linens downstairs to the laundry facilities. The rest of the inn was quiet. Rose sat with Clara and Montgomery in the dining room, but I didn't hear anyone else around. I peeked into the kitchen. Paul Peterson stood at the counter, his back toward me. So, he had returned after Becky and I had seen him in the garage. His actions were leading me to believe he was up to something. Pretentious Paul had become Prying Paul.

"I'm sorry," I said as I stepped into the room, "but you missed breakfast."

Paul slammed a drawer shut and turned to face me. "Um, yeah." He ran his fingers through his carefully mussed-up hair. "Mary overslept and I got caught up in writing the script for the show."

"If you give me a couple minutes, I can find something for you. It won't be as elegant as one of Wil's breakfasts, but it will keep you going until lunch."

"Don't worry about it," he said, walking toward me and the door. "We're on our way out and we'll grab something." He had regained his polished voice. He grinned at me as he passed by through the open door. "We'll try to be on time tomorrow."

"Have a good day." I watched as he went past the

reception desk and then I heard his footsteps on the stairs.

Wil wasn't in the kitchen, so what had Paul been doing there?

The long prep counter was Wil's baby, with a polished stainless-steel top and drawers along both sides. Shelves below the drawers held pans, bowls, and other cooking paraphernalia. Where Paul had been standing, the drawer was partially open. I went over to push it closed, but it was stuck. Kitchen drawers did that all the time, didn't they?

I pulled the drawer open, thinking I only needed to rearrange the utensils inside, but the only item in the drawer was a laptop computer. I wiggled the drawer a bit and it went back on its track and slid closed. Paul must have tried to shove it in at an angle when I surprised him. Had he been trying to gain access to Wil's recipes? If so, he hadn't been successful. But I couldn't figure out why else he would have been poking around in the kitchen.

I took the load of laundry across the hall and started the washer, then checked the list on the wall by the door to make sure I had done all the tasks assigned to me. On the wall above the list was a row of hooks with keys on them. A key fob for Rose's Land Cruiser, then another one for Wil's Prius. The next hook held one of the inn's master keys, identical to the one in my pocket.

I reached for it, then stopped myself, thinking of fingerprints. The utility room was accessible to anyone at any time. The hall outside the door led from the garage, past this room and kitchen, and on to the reception area. Anyone could have grabbed this key, put Dead Dick in my room, and returned it...and they could have done it without any of us seeing them. I slipped into the kitchen and found a plastic bag. Inverting it over my hand, I grasped the key and sealed it inside the bag.

Had Paul found the accessible master key during his snooping? But he hadn't checked in until after Dead Dick had been planted in my room.

A quick check of the list told me I was free until after lunch, so I went to Rose's suite and started gathering my things to move them upstairs. Thatcher followed every step, from Rose's bathroom to the kitchen, and then to my briefcase. I rubbed the dog's ears then picked up Tim's traveling crate where the cat lay with his front paws tucked under his chest watching every move the corgi made.

"Are you making sure I get everything?" I asked. The little dog rolled over on his back so I could rub his tummy. "Admit it, you'll miss having Tim around."

Thatcher's tongue hung from the side of his mouth as his bright brown eyes watched my face, listening. I'm sure he could understand every word I said.

"You can come upstairs and visit him whenever you want."

I gave Thatcher a final pat, then grabbed the handle of Tim's carrier in one hand and my canvas briefcase in the other.

Unpacking only took a few minutes and Tim quickly settled in after I filled his food and water bowls. I put the master key I had found on my kitchen counter and called Cal.

"What's up?"

I grinned as I recognized my own greeting. "Is that

how you always answer the phone?"

"When it's someone I know."

"So, that means that you put my name in your contacts list."

After a moment of silence, he said, "You're a pretty good detective. But back to my first question – what's up?"

"I found a master key for the inn on a hook in the laundry room. Anyone could have used it."

"Is it still there?"

"I have it. And don't worry. I bagged it so I wouldn't disturb any fingerprints."

"Okay. I'll stop by and pick it up when I get a chance. It might not be until tomorrow."

"That's fine."

I ended the call and stared at Cal's name on my contact list. I had added his name because I didn't like to answer calls from unknown numbers. But why would he add my name to his list? Maybe we were more alike than I had thought.

Sitting on the sectional in my living room, I propped my stockinged feet on the ottoman and closed my burning eyes. Between the time change, my new schedule, and spending short nights on Rose's couch, I was exhausted. But knowing that there was a murderer on the loose kept my mind swirling with the details. The key. Rose quartz.

I needed some time with my bullet journal to get all these thoughts down on paper.

I took the notebook and my favorite pens from my bag and opened to a fresh page. I started listing all the details filling my brain.

Across the top of the page, I wrote "suspects." The next column was "clues." The third was "questions."

Under the clues title, I listed everything I had found or thought about in the last few days. The key topped the list. I moved to the questions column and in block lettering I wrote, "Master key? Who had access?" Then I went back to the list of clues. I had nothing more to add.

In the suspects column I listed the names. Everyone connected with the inn. Then back to the questions.

I wrote: "Who wanted Dick Brill dead?" The next question came immediately: "And why?"

Tuesday's breakfast was a success, even though Becky had been late with her delivery. I followed her into the kitchen after bringing copies of the local newspaper in.

Wil glanced at her and emitted a low growl that sounded a lot like Thatcher. "Where have you been?"

"You wanted sourdough loaves baked fresh this morning, and that takes time. Especially when you added two loaves of challah at the last minute."

Becky dropped the tray of bread on the counter with a bang.

Wil turned from the griddle where he was making hash browns. "A professional baker would have allowed enough time."

As he turned his back to her, she rolled her eyes, then grinned a hello to me before continuing with the banter.

"A professional chef," she said, "wouldn't have

waited until ten o'clock at night to add to his order."

"I was busy."

"Busy doing what?"

I sipped my coffee, waiting to hear what Wil would say. He hadn't shown up to help set up yesterday afternoon's tea, but Rose and I had carried on without him.

"I had a meeting." He moved the piles of hashbrowns to a waiting pan and slid them into the warming oven.

"Wait a minute," I said, "were those hashbrowns orange?"

"Of course. Sweet potatoes are orange." Wil flicked the light on in another oven and peered into it. "Sweet potato hash browns, French baked eggs, and toasted sourdough bread with maple bacon butter. That's the menu for this morning, along with a fresh fruit plate."

"Then what is the challah for?" Becky asked.

"Tomorrow's breakfast. Day-old challah is the best bread for my Crème Brulée casserole."

"Day old? You're not even eating this beautiful bread today? I should take it back to the café."

Wil chuckled and gave me one of his crooked grins. "I knew that would rile her up."

"You're impossible." Becky shook her head. "I've got the scones out in the car. Come on, Emma, you can help me."

She led the way toward the garage.

"Tell me everything," she said on the way down the hall. "Do you have any suspects for the murder?"

I glanced behind me to make sure no one could hear us. I only heard Wil humming in the kitchen.

"No suspects yet, but I have a couple leads."

"Really?" Becky paused with her hand on the doorknob. "Anything you can share with me?"

Wil's humming had stopped, and I couldn't hear any other sound, but still...

"We can't talk here."

Becky raised her eyebrows but led the way out to her car without another comment. The crisp morning breeze made me wish I had slipped on a jacket.

"What leads?" Becky said as she opened the back hatch.

I thought through the lists in my Bullet Journal. "Pretty slim ones. I need to find out more about the people here at the inn."

"I hope one of them didn't do it."

"It has to be someone connected with the inn. Someone who had access to-" I stopped myself. Becky was at the inn every day. She could go in and out and no one would think twice about it. And she would know about the master key on the hook in the utility room.

"What?" She frowned. "You're staring at me funny."

"You couldn't have done it, could you?"

She laughed, took another look at me, and then laughed again. She took a pastry box out of the SUV and handed it to me. The fragrance of cherries and almonds reached my nose.

"I couldn't murder anyone. I can't even stand to kill the flies that make their way into Gran's kitchen." Holding the second pastry box in one hand, she closed the hatch of the SUV. "Besides, why would I kill Dick? He was a nice guy. We're all going to miss him."

"You knew him?"

"Our whole family did. He was a professor at the university, taught community education courses, gave lectures, and guided tours. He ate at Gran's Café every time he was near Paragon." She leaned against the car. "He always ordered the same thing. Gran's hero sandwich and fries."

"When was the last time he ate at the café?"

"He was there on Thursday for lunch."

"Last Thursday?" I counted back. Today was Tuesday. "That was five days ago. We found his body on Friday."

"Could Thursday have been the day he was killed?" She shivered and stepped closer to me. "Do you think he left the café, came up here, and-" Becky blinked fast, as if she was holding back tears.

I squeezed her arm. "You really did like him, didn't you?"

"Yeah." She looked at me and nodded. "Yeah, I did. You don't meet truly nice guys like him very often."

"If he was that nice, who would want to kill him?"

She shrugged. "Maybe he was just in the wrong place at the wrong time."

"Somewhere with rose quartz."

"Rose quartz?"

"Cal said that the murder weapon was a piece of rose quartz. The coroner found bits of it in the wound."

Becky indicated the pine-covered mountains surrounding us with her free hand. "There is quartz all around us. You can't go anywhere without stumbling over a piece."

I chewed my bottom lip. "Maybe it was an accident? Could he have fallen and hit his head on a rock?"

"But then how did he end up in your suite?" Becky shook her head. "If this was an accident, he'd still be lying up there in the forest somewhere."

"That takes us right back to an unknown murderer, and probably someone with connections to the inn."

"Well, it had better not be Wil," Becky said as she started toward the garage door. "He's just too much fun to tease every morning."

"That's what you call it? Teasing?" I grabbed the morning paper from the edge of the driveway as I followed her through the garage. "You two bicker like ducks after the same June bug."

"He is pretty cute, though, even with all of his stubborn pride."

"Someone has a crush on the chef," I said in a singsong.

Becky shushed me as we walked down that hall to the kitchen. "Don't you dare repeat that to anyone!"

"Don't worry." I grinned at her worried look. "I promise. I won't mention it."

I poured myself a fresh cup of coffee after Becky left and went out to the dining room to set up for breakfast. Montgomery was the first one downstairs. He tucked a copy of the paper under his arm.

"What's on the menu today?" he asked as he made a cup of tea for himself.

I told him, and when I got to the maple bacon butter, he sucked in a breath.

"Oh, my, that sounds delicious." He patted his flat stomach. "I'm going to put on weight if I spend much more time here. Wil's cooking is exquisite."

"It's to-" I stopped myself. I couldn't say that it

was "to die for" anymore. Not since Dead Dick had shown up in my living room. "It is good, isn't it? Wil is very talented."

Montgomery stroked his mustache. "Talented, yes. Rose was lucky to have found him. I understand they're business partners."

"That's what Rose told me."

"He's a young man, isn't he? Doesn't it make you wonder where he got the capital to invest in a place like this?"

I glanced at the closed shutter between the dining room and kitchen as I set up the chafing rack. I hoped our voices weren't carrying through it to Wil's ears. "I hadn't thought about it. Rose said she was the senior partner, so I assumed his contribution to the business was more talent than money."

"That could be." He stirred his tea. "Or perhaps he inherited his money."

"Maybe." This line of thought didn't seem important, and it was time to change the subject. I set a stack of clean plates on the buffet. "You've been up to the mine, haven't you?"

"A few times."

I turned toward Montgomery, but he was focused on the morning headlines. Or he seemed to be.

Giving my voice a casual tone, I said, "Have you ever seen any rose quartz up there?"

"Hmm?" He sipped his tea. "Rose quartz? I'm not sure I'd know what it was if I saw it. Why?"

"I heard someone mention it and I thought I'd like to look for a piece. It sounds like it could be a beautiful stone."

Montgomery's pleasant expression turned grim. "Emma, don't go poking around up there. It isn't safe."

"Rose said-"

"I don't mean the mine isn't safe. I mean that you might get mixed up in something you don't want to be involved in."

I sat at the table across from him. "Is something going on that Rose should know about?"

He frowned. "Rose knows as much as she needs to. Just take my advice and stay away from the mine."

Annie and Roger came down the stairs right then, followed by Paul and Mary, so I didn't get a chance to ask Montgomery what he thought was going on. Wil opened the shutter over the buffet and set a pan of eggs in the chafing rack while I set up the toaster and slid in four slices of sourdough bread.

Wil leaned on the counter across from me, dropping his voice to nearly a whisper. "What was Montgomery saying about the mine?"

I glanced at Montgomery. He still held the newspaper in front of him but seemed to be watching Rose's door.

"He said it wasn't safe up there, and that I should stay away from it."

"He's right. An old mine isn't a place to go exploring. You never know when a shaft might cave in."

I took out the toasted bread, set it in a basket, and put four more slices in.

"Rose said the mine itself is safe enough, but Montgomery seemed to think there was something going on up there."

Wil's crooked grin disappeared, replaced by a frown. "The old guy has a screw loose. What could be going on at an abandoned mine?"

"Other than Paul's ghost chasing show?"

His frown deepened. "They aren't really going to film an episode in that mine, are they?"

"It would be exciting, wouldn't it? And it would be great publicity for the inn."

A timer rang in the kitchen.

"That's not the kind of publicity we need," he said, pushing himself away from the counter. "We don't have any trouble bringing in customers, thanks to my cooking."

The toaster popped. I put the hot slices into the basket and slid it along the buffet. The two couples were serving themselves their breakfasts and Montgomery still sat alone at his table. He wasn't even pretending to read the newspaper anymore but stood when Rose's door opened and she came out with Thatcher.

"I say, dear Rose," he said, crossing the dining room toward her, "I think I'll join you on your walk this morning, if you don't mind."

I missed what she said in response, but she must have agreed because they walked out the door together just as Clara came out of her room. She paused to watch, then came over to me.

"Montgomery is walking the dog with Rose this morning?" She stopped next to me, her arms crossed. "That's odd."

"Not if he's interested in her."

Clara gave me a blank look.

"I mean in a romantic way. You know, sweet on her."

"Montgomery Reynolds? Sweet on Rose? Nay, I don't think so."

"Why not?"

Clara gave me an appraising look, her eyes narrowed. "Have you had breakfast yet?"

"Not yet."

"Come join me this morning."

I freshened my coffee, served myself some fruit salad, and joined Clara at a table at the far end of the dining room. I wasn't sure she could be more obvious in her desire for privacy, but the other diners weren't paying attention to us.

"In the old days," Clara said while she buttered her toast, "Montgomery was quite a ladies' man. Thought of himself as some James Bond, but handsome is as handsome does."

"You knew him from before?"

She nodded. "Rose did, too. We all worked together." She took a bite of her toast.

I leaned forward. "What kind of work did you do?"

"That isn't important." She brushed some crumbs off her fingers. "This toast is delicious, and the butter is the perfect spread for it. Wil is a right canny cook, aye?"

I ignored her attempt to change the subject. "What do you mean, that he was a ladies' man?"

Clara rolled her eyes. "Women." She held up a hand in denial. "But not me. I was only an office worker. And I don't think Rose was ever one of his bonnie lasses. She was too devoted to Harry, even after his death."

"But that was a long time ago. You don't think her feelings might have changed?"

"Not toward Montgomery. Their interest in each other is only professional."

Clara took a bite of the sweet potato hash browns

on her fork and ate it with her eyes closed in bliss. She must have meant 'was professional.' They were both retired, weren't they?

"Why do you think he wanted to walk Thatcher with her this morning?"

Chewing, Clara didn't answer right away. "I wonder," she said.

"You wonder what?"

She stared at the door as if she could see through it. "Could Montgomery have found something?"

I wondered if sweet Clara could be going senile. "Found something? About what?"

Clara shook herself slightly, then turned toward me with a warm smile.

"Oh, don't mind me, dear. My imagination can take me places that don't make sense sometimes." She cut into her French baked eggs with her fork. "This breakfast is delicious. Wil should write a cookbook so we can take these recipes home with us."

"That's a good idea. I'll have to ask him what he thinks about it." I rose from the table. "I need to freshen the buffet. I hear Sam and Nora coming downstairs."

"Oh, yes dear. Rose and Montgomery will be returning soon, also."

As I went toward the kitchen, Clara pulled a book out of her bag and opened it. In spite of her sometimes-befuddled expression, talking to her had been a pleasure. I was beginning to see why she and Rose were such good friends.

"Wil," I said as I put more slices of bread in the toaster, but I stopped when I looked across the counter. The kitchen was empty. I went into the hall and opened the door to the utility room. No Wil.

Next, I checked the garage. He wasn't there, either.

"If he's going to disappear, he had better not get mad at me for invading his kitchen," I muttered as I grabbed some hot pads off the counter and took the pan of eggs out of the warmer.

By the time I had put the fresh batch of eggs in the chafing rack and sliced another loaf of bread for toast, Rose and Montgomery were back from their walk. Rose made herself a cup of tea and sat at the table with Clara while Montgomery filled his plate at the buffet. Sam and Nora were sitting by themselves, and the other two couples were still talking. I heard Paul mention the mine, but other than that I couldn't hear what they were talking about.

I stood at my favorite spot at the end of the counter, sipping a fresh cup of coffee and thinking about Dick. Why would any of the people in this room want to see him dead?

Sam ate quickly, shoveling his food into his mouth and not even looking at his wife. Nora, on the other hand, sat back in her chair, pushing her potatoes around on her plate with her fork. She didn't look at her husband, either. Had the two of them had a fight? They certainly spent a lot of time bickering. They were on my list of suspects, although I didn't have enough information to pinpoint a motive.

Annie had shifted her chair closer to Paul's and Roger didn't seem to have noticed. I had a good view of her face. The giddy fangirl was gone. She leaned close to Paul and laid one hand on his knee. Her expression? Knowing. That's how I had to describe it. She didn't look like a girl talking to a celebrity, but like a woman talking to someone she knew well. Then Roger and Mary laughed about something, and

Annie's brief look was gone. She turned toward Roger and the intimate moment was over...if it had ever happened. My imagination was working overtime.

Could Dick have gotten wind of Paul's plans to film an episode of his show at the mine and objected to it? Would that be enough of a motive for murder? Or were Annie and Roger a couple of those super-fans you hear about sometimes, who would do anything for their favorite hero?

I glanced at Rose and Clara, chatting about their memories of someone named Ruth. It sounded like they had known this other woman in college. Neither one of them had killed Dick. I was sure of it.

But what about Montgomery? He had set his plate on Rose's and Clara's table and had made himself a cup of tea. Joining them, he lifted his teacup in a toast. On Friday afternoon, he had said he was writing a book, but he hadn't mentioned it since. Could that have been a cover for something else? But what? And what connection could it possibly have with Dead Dick? I thought of my mnemonic for him - he certainly was mysterious. Mysterious Montgomery couldn't be the murderer, could he? Then I remembered how quickly his expression had changed when I mentioned going up to the mine. Underneath his kind exterior, there was another Montgomery. Grim at times, and also ruthless? Maybe.

I closed my eyes and rubbed my temples. I had my list of suspects, but I couldn't imagine which one might be a murderer.

.

Six

"Hey, girl."

I was on my hands and knees in the upstairs lounge, shoving the vacuum's wand attachment under the couch in search of dust bunnies, but Becky's greeting gave me an excuse to turn off the machine. I dusted off my knees and grinned at her.

"You brought a friend," I said, nodding at the corgi that followed her.

She patted her knee and rubbed Thatcher's ears as he bounded up to her. "He knows I always carry dog treats in my pocket." She gave him a tidbit, then held up a piece of poster board. "Jeremy had this leftover from a school project. I thought we could use it to make a crime board."

"Which one is Jeremy?"

"The nine-year-old. He has a cowlick right here." She pointed to the crown of her head.

"I remember him. He was wearing an Avengers tee at church."

"He's the one. Anyway, here's the poster board. Do you want to do it?"

"Like on television? Where they put the victim's

picture up and then string pieces of yarn to connect the suspects with him?"

"That's right."

"Sounds like a good idea. I need a visual to help organize all the competing thoughts in my head." I started winding up the vacuum cord. "My journal is great for lists, but we need something that helps us see the big picture."

Becky held up the poster board. "Like this."

"Exactly. Go on into my suite while I put the vacuum away. Tim is in there, and he loves company."

By the time I got back to my rooms, Thatcher was snuggled on the couch next to Becky with his feet in the air. Tim perched on the back, kneading his paws in the upholstery. He looked at me, his eyes half-closed.

"You've got yourself a couple of friends."

Becky scratched Tim's white fleck. "Thatcher loves to cuddle, but Tim seems pretty happy to be at a distance."

"That's his style. I'll get out my pens and we can start."

Becky had laid the poster board on the ottoman, and it fit perfectly.

"What are we going to use for the pictures?"

"For now, let's just draw a box and write in the person's name. We might be able to get a photo of Dick from the newspaper."

"Or from the university website." Becky scooted forward and held the poster board still while I drew a rectangle in the center and wrote Dick's name. When I finished, she said, "Okay. Now, who are our suspects?"

I opened my bullet journal to the list I had made yesterday. "All the guests at the inn, to begin with."

We took turns drawing the rectangles around the perimeter of the board and writing in the names.

When we finished, I added the few details I had learned about each guest while observing them that morning. When I got to Annie, I tapped the pen on the poster board. That look on Annie's face at breakfast had told me she and Paul had a history. But when? And where? And did Roger know about it?

"We need a timeline," I said. "Can we use the back of the board?"

Becky flipped the cardboard over. "Why a timeline?"

"There are too many details getting clobbered up in my mind." I drew a line across the center of the board. I put a tick mark in the middle. "I'll put finding Dick's body here, then we can fill in what happened before and after." I wrote in the time and day.

"Okay." Becky pointed to about twelve inches to the left of the murder. "This spot can be Thursday noon. We know he had lunch at the café."

I wrote in the information.

"We know where Dick was at noon on Thursday, and we know he was dead by Friday afternoon. So can we put in a time of death here?" Becky tapped the spot between the two events.

"Not yet." I put the cap on my marker. "We don't have an exact time of death for him."

I turned to the list of questions in my bullet journal.

"What else do we know that we can put on here?" Becky asked.

"We know when each of the guests arrived at the inn."

"Do you have different color markers? We could color-code each person."

"That's a great idea. We have twenty-four colors to use, but I hope we don't end up with that many suspects."

I filled in the arrival of the guests, all on Friday before I found Dick's body.

"How detailed do we want to get? I mean, should we write in everyone's movements since they arrived?"

"That can get pretty complex in a hurry." I tapped the brown marker I had used for Mysterious Montgomery on the poster board. "How about if we only write down the things that stand out?"

"Like when we found Paul in the garage?"

"Exactly. And later that morning when I found him in the kitchen." I wrote down those two instances, using purple for Pretentious Paul. "What was he really doing there? Was he looking for something?"

"That sounds like another question for your journal."

I wrote it on the page, then turned back to the timeline. "There are too many questions. We don't know why Dick was in Paragon on Thursday. We don't know why Paul was snooping around. And I don't know why Mysterious Montgomery is so mysterious."

"What do you mean?"

I filled Becky in on my conversation with Clara. "But I don't know Clara well enough to know if what she says is accurate. He seems to be what he says, but

Clara painted a different picture of him. I wonder if her mind could be slipping."

"You mean like dementia?" Becky frowned. "I would hate to see that happen. She and Rose are friends from way back, aren't they?"

"That's what I understand. Maybe I should ask Rose about her."

Becky looked at her watch. "I need to get going. The schools only have a half-day today, and I'm on kid patrol until their parents get home from work."

We left the crime board on the ottoman and Tim asleep on the back of the couch, his front feet tucked under his chest. Thatcher followed us down the stairs.

"I'll see you in the morning," Becky said as she went out the front door.

I went in search of Rose. The dining room and library were empty. I didn't want to disturb Rose if she was working on her memoirs, so I swung open the kitchen door. Wil stood at his prep counter with his back to me, his computer open as he made notes on a spread sheet. Before I saw any more, Wil slammed his laptop shut and turned toward me.

"What are you doing here?"

"Have you seen Rose?" I asked. Thatcher pushed past me, trotted over to Wil, and jumped up on his leg.

Wil pushed him away, but Thatcher growled and grabbed the hem of Wil's jeans in his teeth.

"Thatcher," I said, snatching him from the floor. "What do you think you're doing?"

"That dog is crazy. He shouldn't be in the kitchen anyway." Wil slid the computer into the drawer of his prep table. "What do you want?"

"Do you know where Rose is?"

"She might be in the greenhouse. I think I saw her go out there a while ago."

What a grump, I thought as I carried Thatcher down the corridor toward the garage.

I rubbed the dog's ears before I set him on the garage floor.

"What has gotten into you? Why did you go after Wil like that?"

Thatcher looked up at me, his hind end wiggling, and winked one eye.

I bent over and scratched him under his chin. "If I didn't know better, I'd think you were trying to tell me something."

He circled through the over-sized garage and stopped at some sort of two-wheeled cart that was hanging on the far wall. He sniffed at the tires, then gruffed.

"What is that?" I joined Thatcher. The cart was little more than a frame on two wheels, about six feet long. It was almost like a wheelchair, but instead of a seat it had a frame that reclined. I had never seen anything like it before. Something else to ask Rose.

"Is this what you were trying to tell me?"

Thatcher's hind end wagged, but he still sniffed the cart's frame carefully. Then he looked at me again and woofed.

I rubbed his ears. "I'm sorry, I don't speak dog."

Thatcher stared at me and winked again.

I gave him a final pat. "Okay, if you're so smart, go find Rose."

He trotted to the door leading through the back of the garage, his nose to the floor. Through the door's window I could see the interior of the greenhouse and Rose moving among the plants.

"Good dog," I said as I opened the door, letting Thatcher run through ahead of me.

When Rose saw us, she put down her trimmers and took off her gloves.

"Well," she said as she ruffled Thatcher's fur. "You finally made it out to the greenhouse."

"I think I would almost call it a conservatory," I said.

The greenhouse was as large as the spacious garage, with the half to my right filled with raised beds full of vegetables separated by narrow aisles. In the center a couple patio chairs sat near a small fountain. Then on my left, against the wall of the inn, were leafy plants. Along the outside wall flowers were growing in beds. The air was heady with competing fragrances.

"When you told me about this place, I had no idea it would be so extensive." I indicated the leafy plants. "What are those?"

Rose led the way to the chairs near the fountain. "They are my pride and joy. Tea plants, three different varieties. The beds over along the far wall are chamomile, both German and Roman. In the gardens outside I have roses for rose hips, lavender, mint, and other herbs."

"You blend your teas from these plants?"

She nodded as she rubbed Thatcher's ears. "South Dakota isn't the best place to grow tea, so we buy the teas we serve in the inn from a local blender. This hobby is for my enjoyment, and I do harvest a few leaves for my own use now and again."

"Where did you learn how to grow the tea?"

"When we were in India. Harry and I lived on a tea plantation, and I learned from the manager there."

Thatcher snooped around the base of the fountain, and Rose leaned back in her chair, smiling at the memories. "That was years ago, of course, but since then I have wanted to grow my own tea and the inn has given me that opportunity."

She seemed to want to talk about the past and I saw my opening. "You and Clara were friends even back then, weren't you?"

"Oh, my, of course. The two of us have been best friends since early days. We were both students at the same boarding school, and then went on to the same college. We even had a crush on the same boy our freshman year." Her face grew soft as she looked beyond the walls of the greenhouse and back through the years. "I ended up marrying him, but Clara never held it against me."

"That was Uncle Harry?"

Rose brought her gaze back to me and the present. "Yes. Your father looked a lot like him, you know. The Blackwood men were both quite handsome."

"What did Clara do after she graduated?"

"She didn't graduate." Rose's smile disappeared. "Her mother passed away the fall of our junior year and she had to quit school to raise her younger brothers and sisters. I've never heard her complain about it, although I know she was disappointed. The rest of us went on to have careers in the business, and Clara was hired to work in the office once her youngest sister went to school. She was a valuable asset, but I know she would rather have been in the field."

I wanted to ask what business they had been in, but I couldn't lose track of my goal. "Clara said something about Montgomery working with you and

Uncle Harry back then."

"She did?"

"When she told me, I wasn't sure if she was, well, telling me a story." I laughed a little under Rose's scrutiny. "She said that Montgomery had been quite a ladies' man."

Rose smiled, but it didn't extend to her eyes. "Clara does have an imagination."

"You didn't work with Montgomery?"

She pulled her gardening gloves off. "Did anyone else hear what she was saying?"

"We were sitting at the far end of the room, and she spoke so softly I had trouble hearing her."

Rose straightened each finger on the left glove, then did the same to the right one. I waited. If she wanted to tell me more, she would.

"Will you do me a favor and forget anything Clara said?" Rose sighed. "When the time is right, I'll tell you everything." She looked at me again. "Do you mind?"

My curiosity almost made me blurt out another question, but Rose's confidential attitude made me pause.

"I can keep a secret, don't worry." I shifted a little closer to her. "Do you know what that little cart is in the garage?"

"Cart?"

"It's made out of metal and is hanging on the wall. It almost looks like a recliner or chair to transport someone."

"Oh, yes. That's Wil's game cart. He likes to hunt, and he uses that to carry deer back from the forest."

"I thought hunters just carried their carcasses out of the woods slung over their shoulders."

"A mule deer buck can weigh as much as a man. Most hunters use one of those carts."

After my encounter with Wil a few minutes ago, it didn't take much for me to imagine him shooting a deer and bringing it home.

Thatcher came back to Rose, and she lifted him onto her lap. He sat with his eyes half-closed, his tongue hanging out in a happy smile as she rubbed his furry white chest.

"How are you and Wil getting along?" she asked.

"He's a bit temperamental, isn't he?"

Rose frowned. "He never has been before, but I've noticed it, too, since I got home from Arizona last month."

"Becky says it's his super-chef personality."

"Like on one of those television cooking shows?" Rose chuckled. "I wouldn't say that. He is brilliant, of course, but he's always kept a level head."

A frown passed over her face.

"Until this year?"

She sighed. "Maybe it's a passing thing. I hope he isn't thinking of moving on with his career."

"Why would he even consider it? He has a dream position here."

"He's a big-city personality in a small town. He usually travels during the winter while the inn is closed, but he stayed in Paragon this year."

"It must have been lonely for him."

"It's a funny thing. Sometime in January, he called me. He offered to buy my share of the inn."

"But this is your inn. You wouldn't sell it, would you?"

"Oh, no." She laughed and waved the idea away. "This is my life now. I couldn't give it up."

"That's good. I haven't been here long, but I can't imagine this place without your presence." I checked my watch. "It's time for me to set up for tea."

"All of these guests are staying through the week, aren't they?"

"Yes, that's right. The Smiths and the Nelsons plan to check out on Saturday morning. Clara is staying on, of course, as well as Paul and Mary. Is Montgomery here next week, also?"

"He'll be here for another couple weeks. And next week we'll have Paul Peterson's filming crew here."

"Another full week. It should be fun."

As I walked back through the garage, I realized that if the murderer was connected with the inn, they could very well be leaving by the end of the week. Could Cal and I find the killer before they left town? I counted on my fingers. We had a little more than three days before the Smiths and Nelsons planned to check out, and then our suspects would start scattering.

After I had everything ready for tea, I walked down the hill to the mailbox at the end of Graves' Gulch Road. I tucked the few bills under my arm and examined the envelope addressed to Rose. The words were typed and there was no return address on the envelope. The stamp had a smudge of ink on it, but it was so blurry I couldn't make out the postmark.

When I got back to the reception desk, I put the mail in Rose's basket just as Roger and Annie came in the front door and went up to their room to change out of their hiking clothes. Sam and Nora were right behind them, followed by Paul and Mary.

Afternoon tea was a lively affair. Paul and Mary had spent the day researching ghost stories in the area and as the rest of the guests enjoyed their refreshments, Paul held us all spellbound as he told one of the tales in his trademark Ghost Chaser voice. When he reached the end, he bowed, and his audience applauded enthusiastically.

"That was marvelous," said Roger, sitting in his chair after adding a standing ovation to his applause.

"Just like watching your show," Nora said. She had listened with her mouth open, her scone forgotten on her plate. "Is that the story you'll be using for this episode?"

"How can he?" Sam pushed his legs out in front of him and crossed them at the ankles. "That story took place after a stage robbery, not a mine cave-in."

Paul grinned. "That's the magic of television. I can make the story take place anywhere I want to."

Mary broke in. "Paul, we have a dinner reservation in Rapid City. We need to leave soon to make it there in time."

"I need to change my clothes first," Paul said. "I'll meet you in the car."

Annie turned to her husband. "I left my purse upstairs. You go ahead to the car, and I'll be there in a minute."

As Annie followed Paul up the stairs, the rest of the group headed for the front door, chatting about Paul's ghost story. Clara and Rose sat at their table while I started clearing the tea cups and plates. I couldn't keep my mind off the two who had gone upstairs. Did Annie and Paul know each other as well as it had seemed at breakfast?

I put my tray down and started up the steps. If anyone asked, I could say that I just wanted to check on Tim. Before I reached the landing, I heard voices.

Paul's deep tones were easy to recognize, and the woman's voice had to be Annie's. It sounded like they were in the corridor outside Roger and Annie's room, speaking very quietly. I turned to go back down the steps, but then Annie's voice rose.

"Paul, you promised. After graduation, you said you would find me, but I never heard from you."

"I was a professor, and you were a student. I couldn't risk my job."

"You were a visiting professor. They wouldn't have done anything to you." Silence. Then Annie continued. "I gave the baby up for adoption. You had a daughter."

My fingers curled on the banister.

Paul snorted. "I never believed it was mine, anyway."

"You know I loved you and only you, and I could never hurt our baby."

"You should have just gotten an abortion and been done with it."

She sucked in a hissing breath. "I could kill you saying that."

Annie's words sent a chill through me. Her voice was as hard and cold as ice. I went back down the steps and took the dishes into the kitchen. I mentally kicked myself for eavesdropping. No snoop ever heard anything that was good for them.

Even though I spent an hour rereading one of my favorite books that night, as midnight approached, I was still wide awake. I took a warm shower and put on my favorite flannel pajamas, but I couldn't stay in bed. Tim watched me pace through the living room from the doors leading out onto the deck to the kitchen alcove and back. Finally, I sat on the sofa with my feet up and he stalked over to snuggle on my lap.

When I rubbed his ears, he purred and he licked my fingers in response, then reached one paw up to bat at my chin. His eyes half-closed as I scratched the white spot on his chest.

There were too many suspects, that was the problem. How did Cal ever sort through all the evidence in a case and come up with a conclusion? Any one of the people on the crime board could have murdered Dick. But despite everything I was learning about them, I still couldn't imagine any of them actually committing the crime.

My head throbbed. A glance at the microwave in my little kitchen told me that there were only a few hours left in my short night. Five o'clock was going to be here way too soon. I went into my bedroom, took off my robe and laid it across the end of my bed, then slipped between the sheets. So comfortable, so quiet, so...

I was almost asleep when a crashing sound from downstairs made me sit up in bed.

"What in the world?"

I threw on my robe and ran downstairs before thinking what I might be heading into. I flipped on the main floor lights and saw someone go into the kitchen, leaving the door swinging on its two-way hinge. I grabbed the letter opener off the reception desk.

"Who's there?" I took a step toward the dining room and righted an overturned chair. "You there, in the kitchen. What are you doing?"

There was no reply, and no sound other than Thatcher's frantic barking from Rose's suite.

I took three steps down the hall and pushed on the kitchen door. It swung back toward me, gaining speed and strength as it crushed me against the wall. A tall form ran past toward the front door.

He reached the entrance just as I rounded the corner from the hall by the reception desk. He had left the front door open. I followed him as far as the front porch. The intruder was gone. Disappeared.

Man, my nose hurt. I touched it and felt blood.

"What is going on?" Rose asked, coming out the door behind me. Thatcher ran past her and down the driveway, barking.

"There was an intruder, but he ran out the door before I could stop him."

Blood from my nose dripped on the cement at my feet. That's when I realized I was barefoot and freezing.

"Let's go back inside and take care of your wounds."

Rose turned me around. Clara was in the entry wearing her pink chenille robe. She took one look at me and grabbed the box of tissues we kept at the reception desk. I pulled out three or four and held them to my nose as Montgomery came down the stairs.

"What is happening?"

"It seems we had an intruder," Rose said. She went back to the front door to call the corgi in. "Thatcher followed him all the way down driveway."

Through the open door, I saw Thatcher trotting toward us, occasionally turning around to woof in the direction of the main road.

Montgomery pulled Rose back into the inn and closed the door behind Thatcher. "He probably had a car waiting for him at the bottom of the hill, otherwise Thatcher would still be chasing him." He patted the dog's head, then looked at me. "Did you see him? Can you describe him?"

"He wore a dargk hoodie," I said, holding my sore nose and trying to stop the bleeding. "He wad in de kidchen. Wad would he wandt from dere?"

Rose frowned at me. "You need to sit down, and I'll get an ice pack. Meanwhile," she said, turning to the others, "Emma's right. What would be in the kitchen that's worth stealing?"

Seven

B y the time my nose stopped bleeding, Cal had arrived to investigate.

"Do you people ever sleep?" His voice came out as a growl, but his eyes held a look of concern when he saw me. "What happened to you?"

"The intruder banged the kitchen door into me." I touched my nose. "I don't think it's broken."

"It's going to leave a nasty bruise." Cal took a kit from his duffel and pulled out a small flashlight. He shined it in my right eye, and then the left. "Doesn't look like you have a concussion." He touched my nose, pressing on it until I yelped. "And your nose isn't broken."

"And now you're a medic?"

Cal put the flashlight back in the kit and put it in his duffel. "EMT training." He turned to Rose. "Can you tell me what happened?"

"Emma heard the intruder first."

"He knocked a chair over."

Cal raised a hand to shush me. "You'll have your turn. Go on, Rose."

"As far as we can tell, he went into the kitchen. He

wasn't there very long, maybe a minute?" She looked at me for confirmation and I nodded. "Then he ran through the kitchen door, knocking Emma against the wall, and out the front entrance."

"Is anything missing?" Cal asked as he took notes.

"I didn't see that anything was gone." Rose looked at the rest of us, but we all shook our heads. "Wil would know better than any of us."

"Where is Wil?" Montgomery asked.

While Rose had been talking, he had moved closer to her, and now stood just behind her and to the side. His position reminded me of a bodyguard.

I looked at the clock above the reception desk. "He should be downstairs any minute now. It's almost five o'clock."

My head throbbed. Between the ache in my nose and my lack of sleep, I was miserable. But the thought of Wil making his magic coffee before too long cheered me up.

"I'll check out the kitchen," Cal said as he glanced at his notes. "Was the front door locked?"

Rose nodded. "I locked it myself last night."

"Then how did he get in?" I asked.

"Or was he here already?" Cal took a toothpick from his shirt pocket and stuck it in his mouth. "Maybe it was one of your guests. Or even one of you." He looked at me.

"That is ridiculous. Why would I bang myself in the nose?" I looked to Rose for support. "You saw him run out the front door, didn't you?"

Rose frowned. "I didn't see anyone, but Thatcher chased someone away."

Cal's answer to that was a grunt. He headed into the kitchen.

Clara was the first to interrupt our impromptu gathering with a yawn. "I'm going to try to get in another hour of sleep. I've never been an early riser, and I'm not about to start now."

Montgomery touched Rose's shoulder. "What do you think? Did Emma surprise an intruder?"

"Of course. There is no reason for Emma to be anything but truthful with us."

"You're sure?" Mysterious Monty's eyes narrowed.

Rose laughed. "I'm sorry, Emma. Montgomery can be quite protective of me."

I looked from Rose to Montgomery and back again, feeling like I was missing a big chunk of the conversation. Just then, Wil came into the kitchen hallway from the garage dressed in his chef whites. He stopped when he saw us.

"What's going on?"

"There was an intruder in the inn early this morning," Rose said. "You didn't hear anything?"

"No." He took a step closer to the kitchen door. "Did he steal anything?"

Cal opened the kitchen door. "That's what I'd like you to tell me." He propped the door open and motioned for all of us to come into the kitchen. "As you can see, the intruder left a trail."

Cal pointed to the drawer on Wil's prep table. It was the same drawer I had caught Paul snooping in on Monday. It had been left open, and it was empty.

"My laptop," Wil said. He ran a hand across the back of his neck, then crossed over to the drawer.

"Don't touch anything," Cal said. "I haven't dusted for fingerprints yet."

Wil glared at him but didn't touch the drawer. He peered into it, but all of us could tell it was empty.

"Which one of you took it?" Wil's voice rose with anger.

"Control yourself." Rose pointed toward the ceiling. "Remember our guests."

"It's only a laptop." I thought Wil's reaction was a bit strong. "You have everything backed up, don't you?"

He turned on me. "What do you know about it?"

"Nothing. I just figured any recipes or files you had on your laptop would be backed up on the Cloud."

"Recipes." He glanced at Cal, then Rose and Montgomery. His expression was stony. "I guess I overreacted." He gave a forced laugh. "I certainly wouldn't want anyone stealing my recipes."

Cal turned to a new page in his notebook. "Give me the details about your computer, and we'll keep a watch at local pawnshops."

While Wil and Cal talked, Rose spoke into my ear. "You've had quite a morning, already. I can handle your breakfast duties if you want to go back to bed."

That's when I realized I was still wearing my pajamas and robe.

"Thank you, but I'll be okay until after breakfast." I backed into the hallway, out of Wil's and Cal's sight. "I'll run upstairs to shower, but I'll be back down in plenty of time to greet the guests."

"As long as you promise you'll take a nap afterward." Rose's face held a worried frown.

"Don't worry, I will."

I headed upstairs and was back in the kitchen within a half hour. Wil had a cup of coffee already poured and Becky walked in right behind me.

"What's going on?" She set the pastry boxes on

the counter and handed the invoice to me for my signature. "You look like you've been hit by a truck."

"She was wounded when she decided to chase our intruder away single-handedly," Wil said as he put a large rectangular baking dish into the oven.

"Intruder?" Becky looked from me to Wil.

"Someone broke into the inn early this morning." I pointed to my nose. "He gave me this on his way out." I cupped both hands around my coffee cup to warm my cold fingers and took a sip of the rich, black liquid.

Becky's eyes went wide when she saw what Wil was doing. "Is that my Challah bread?"

Wil set the timer on the oven.

"No, it's my Crème Brulée casserole. Nothing is better than day-old Challah for this dish,"

Becky rolled her eyes. "I'm outta here. I can't stand to see that beautiful bread die such an inglorious death."

"Someday you're going to have to try it," Wil said, "then you'll see I'm right."

I took my coffee to the reception desk and waved to Becky as she left for the café. As I sipped the hot brew, I closed my eyes. Wil really did make the best coffee. I forgot everything else as I slowly finished the cup, basking in the early morning quiet.

Montgomery came down the stairs, looking as if he had never lost any sleep in his life.

"Good morning, again," I said. "I haven't gotten the newspapers yet."

"I can bring them in. They're on the front porch?"

"Or the driveway. It's been different every day. Thanks."

He opened the door just as Rose was coming in

with Thatcher. The dog headed right in and jumped up to greet me.

I leaned down to pet him.

"How are you feeling?" Rose asked.

"My nose is tender, but other than that I'm fine." I gave Thatcher a final pat.

"I forgot to check for the mail yesterday," Rose said. "Did you get it?"

"Yes." I reached behind the desk and took the envelopes out of her basket. "There were a few bills, and this."

As I handed her the envelope with the typed address, her face went pale. Montgomery was bringing in the newspapers and she turned to him.

"It's another one," she said, and handed him the envelope.

"Another one?" I asked as Montgomery took a small knife from his pocket and slit the envelope open.

"Nothing you need to be worried about," Montgomery said. He glanced inside the envelope, then turned to Rose. "Can we discuss this in your suite?"

Rose led the way while I finished setting up for breakfast. I didn't have much time to wonder about the mysterious exchange before the rest of the guests came down the stairs.

Sam and Nora headed straight for the buffet and for once they seemed to be a happily married couple. When Sam put an extra helping of the Crème Brulée casserole on his wife's plate, she rewarded him with a kiss on the cheek. Sam grinned at her, then took a second venison sausage patty for himself.

As they sat down, Roger and Annie came down

the stairs, hand in hand.

"Good morning," I said.

They were so wrapped up in each other that I wasn't sure they had heard me.

Roger tugged at Annie's hand, pulling her toward the breakfast buffet. She flashed a smile in my direction as she followed her husband. I propped up my chin with my hand and sighed, watching them. Someday, I thought, maybe a handsome man would look at me the way Roger looked at Annie.

"Are you lost in dreamland?"

I jumped at the voice. Cal. I straightened up before I turned to him.

"I could be. I didn't sleep at all last night."

"How are you feeling? Any concerns about your nose?"

I touched it. The pain seemed to be subsiding. "No, except that no one except Becky has said anything about it. I figured it would be black and blue by now."

He studied my face. "Nope. Just some redness. Maybe you'll get by without any bruising."

"That's a relief. I don't want to go around looking like I've been in a fistfight." He was still staring at me. "What else?"

His face darkened. Was he blushing?

"Oh. Yeah. Well, I thought I'd talk to Wil before I go into the office and file my report, and I want to pick up that master key you're holding for me."

"Wil's in the kitchen. I'll get the key and have it here at the reception desk."

Cal turned toward the hall leading to the kitchen door, then stopped.

"You're sure you are okay?"

"I will be after I get some sleep. I plan to take a nap after breakfast."

He took off his hat. "I thought maybe some food would help. You know. Some protein to help your nose heal."

"Protein."

He turned a shade darker. Yes, he was definitely blushing.

"I'm making a mess of this."

"Of what?"

He glared at me. "Of asking you if you'd like to have dinner with me sometime. Maybe Saturday."

"You mean a date?"

The poor man looked like he was going to be sick. "Yeah. A date."

Now I felt sick. I hadn't been on a date since that disastrous affair on St. Kitts. The reason why the company had decided to down-size me.

"No, not a date." Cal stuck his hat back on his head. "Dates are too much pressure. I couldn't handle it." He whooshed out a breath. "I'll start over."

His hands grasped the edge of the desk as if he was afraid of being swept overboard.

"I'll pick you up at six on Saturday night and we'll go have dinner together. I know a great place in Hill City. What do you say?"

"I don't know." I grinned at him. "Are you allowed to eat supper with murder suspects?"

He grinned back. "As long as it isn't a date."

Cal headed toward the kitchen, and I sank down onto the stool behind the desk. Dinner with Cowboy Cal? What could go wrong? I closed my eyes and smiled. Things could only go right.

After the guests had finished breakfast, I served myself some of the casserole. Was Wil right about the Challah? With my first bite, I had to admit that the chef was a genius. I ate another serving while I cleaned up the dining room.

Rose and Montgomery finally came out of her suite.

"Are the guests all gone for the day?" Montgomery asked.

"Most of them. Paul said he was going up to the mine to plan the filming for his show. Everyone else has gone out, too, except for Clara and Mary. Cal is here, talking with Wil about the break-in."

"Mary didn't go to the mine with Paul?" Rose asked.

"No. She didn't come down for breakfast, either. Paul said she had a headache and was staying in bed for the day."

"Please sit down, dear," Rose said as she took a seat at the table that was set farthest from the stairway. "We have something to tell you."

Montgomery knocked on Clara's door and she joined us. All three of them stared at me.

"What is it?" I tried to keep my imagination under control, but scenarios ran through my head that ranged from Rose's imminent death from a horrible disease to her confession as the murderer.

Then Montgomery pulled the envelope from his pocket and laid it on the table. "This is the fourth note like this that Rose has received."

I opened the envelope and read the printed

message out loud. "I have warned you. Get out before someone else gets theirs." I looked at the faces around the table. "What does it mean?"

"I didn't tell you about the notes earlier because we didn't think it could be connected with the murder," Rose said. "The first three notes came while I was still in Arizona for the winter and when I came home, I had hoped that would be the end of them."

"Were they all as threatening as this one? Did you contact the police?"

Rose exchanged glances with Montgomery.

"Yes, I did," Rose said. "But not the local law enforcement."

I didn't understand. Then Montgomery slid a business card across the table to me.

"The World Intelligence Organization?" I flipped the card over, then back again. "I've never heard of it."

"That's the idea," Montgomery said. "If everyone knew about it, it would be impossible for us to do our work. When Rose first called me in to look at the case, we assumed the threats were from someone she had dealings with during her years with the WIO. But the wording of this one made us consider a different possibility."

"Someone connected with Dick's murder?"

"Possibly," Rose said.

"This sounds like a story that fits better in a spy novel or a movie than here in Paragon." I chewed on my bottom lip, then made myself stop. "I've always wondered what you and Uncle Harry did for a living, but Dad never talked about it."

"It does sound a bit far-fetched, doesn't it?" Clara folded her hands. Her expression was calm and a little vague, but something told me that underneath that mask she might possibly be a very formidable opponent.

My bottom lip was getting sore. "But that doesn't matter as much as the fact that Rose has received this threat, and it sounds like whoever sent it knows about Dick's murder. We need to take it seriously."

"I'm dead serious about the threat." Montgomery patted Rose's hand.

"What do we do now? Should you tell Cal?"

Montgomery stroked his mustache with one hand. "Rose isn't convinced the notes are anything more than a false flag to warn her against writing her memoirs, but we'll bring Cal in soon if they continue."

#

After a long nap and a simple lunch, I browsed through Rose's library and found a copy of one of my favorite Agatha Christie novels, *Peril at End House*. I took it up to my room to read and before I realized it, it was nearly time to get ready for afternoon tea. On my way downstairs, I crossed the lounge to check on Mary. I hadn't heard anything from her all day.

The privacy sign was still hanging from her door lever, the way it had ever since the first night Paul and Mary had arrived at the inn. I hesitated, but concern for Mary's well-being overran my sense of propriety.

"Mary?" I tapped on the door. "Are you okay?"

There was no answer, but as I leaned closer to the door, I could hear a television show. It sounded like an episode of Paul Peterson's Ghost Chaser. If she was well enough to watch television, she must be okay.

Annie and Roger came back from their day of

hiking in good spirits and ready to share pictures of the herd of bison they had seen in Custer State Park. Sam was smiling as Nora showed off the Black Hills gold necklace he had bought her with the day's casino winnings.

"Have you given up on the gold hunt?" Roger asked as Sam sat at the table next to his.

"Why crawl around in dirty caves when you can win big at the craps table?" Sam chuckled as Nora planted a big kiss on his cheek and sat next to him with a glass of iced tea and her plate filled with scones.

"But we decided we should do some sight-seeing tomorrow and give the casinos a rest," she said. "It would be too bad to come all this way and never see Mount Rushmore."

"We met a couple today that gave us the name of a rock-climbing guide, and we're meeting him in an area behind Mount Rushmore on Friday." Roger grabbed Annie's hand and squeezed it. "It will be quite an adventure, won't it?"

Annie smiled but pulled her hand away. "You will have the adventure, but I'm just going to watch. You know I'm afraid of heights."

"You need to face your fears in order to get over them," Roger said, the persuasive teacher in him coming out. "Once you get up there, you will love it."

"Not me. I'll go with you, but I'm keeping my feet on terra firma." Annie looked around the room. "Isn't Paul joining us this afternoon? He was going up to the mine to do some research this morning, but I thought he'd be back by now."

"He's been out all day," I said. "He'll probably be back at any time."

But Paul didn't show up. The two couples left for supper and their evening activities while I cleared away the dishes from tea. Montgomery gave me a hand rather than sitting and talking with the ladies.

"You don't have to do this," I said as I took some teacups from him.

"I can't just sit. If I'm on my feet and moving around, at least I feel like I'm doing something to protect your aunt."

I lowered my voice. "When did these threatening notes start arriving?"

"The first one came in January, the second one in March, and the third in April. That's when she called me."

March was when she had contacted me to ask if I would be willing to work at the Sweetbrier this summer.

"She must have taken them seriously."

"Enough to bring me in."

Rose had just brought a plate of meat and cheese for the four of us to have for our supper when we heard a noise from the lounge upstairs.

"That must be Mary," I said. "I'll see if she needs anything."

I started up the stairs, but Mary was at the top, on her way down. She clutched at her stained sweatshirt with one hand as she stared at me with sunken eyes as if she was pleading for help.

"Are you okay?" I grabbed her arm and led her down to the bench in the reception area. "You look like you're ill."

The others gathered around us.

Rose took one look at Mary and took charge. "Something is very wrong. We need to get her to the hospital right away. Montgomery, you drive."

In less than five minutes, I had run upstairs to get Mary's purse with her identification and personal items. I pushed it through the window of the Land Rover into Rose's hands. The last view I had of Mary were her closed eyes as she leaned her head on Rose's shoulder while Montgomery drove off into the early evening dusk.

"Poor Mary," Clara said as we closed the front door behind them.

"She looked so miserable," I said. "I've never seen someone who looked like they were..." I let my voice trail off. I couldn't continue.

"Like they were so close to death?" Clara finished the sentence for me. "I wonder if she has been poisoned."

"You mean you think someone tried to murder her? Who would do that?"

And there was still no sign of Paul.

Eight

After Rose and Montgomery left, Clara went into her room and I went upstairs, my footsteps loud on the wood staircase. The empty inn had always seemed safe until this evening. I turned on the lamps in the public space.

As I went to close Mary's open door, I saw a plate on her bedside table and a half-eaten scone lying on the floor, surrounded by crumbs. I bent down to clean up the mess before the food drew mice or insects, but the memory of Clara's words stopped me. What if she was right and Mary had been poisoned?

I texted Cal to let him know what had happened.

Then I saw a crumpled note under the bed. I could see that it had been written with a scrawling hand, but part of the note was printed, just like the threatening notes Rose had been receiving. I left it where it was and retreated, closing the door behind me.

Clara came out of her room again when Cal arrived a few minutes later.

Cal looked at me, one eyebrow cocked. "What's up?"

"Rose and Montgomery took Mary to the

hospital," I said.

"She was poisoned," Clara said. "I'm sure of it,"

"Let's not jump to any conclusions until we hear for sure." He turned to me. "You said you had something to show me?"

I led Cal upstairs to Mary's room.

Once we out of earshot of Clara, Cal said, "Tell me what happened."

I stopped outside Mary's door and faced him. "While we were eating supper, Mary came out of her room, but she looked awful. She could hardly walk. Rose took one look at her and decided she needed to go to the hospital."

Cal pulled his radio off his belt. "Which one?"

"I think Rose said Custer."

He nodded and punched in some numbers. I could hear the buzzing of a phone ringing, then Cal turned away from me as he talked. Then he put his phone away.

"They arrived at the hospital about ten minutes ago. The doctor I talked to said that they think she's reacting to something she ate, possibly an allergy or food poisoning."

"Will she recover?"

"He couldn't tell me. But now we know that we're looking for something she might have eaten in the past twenty-four hours."

"That's what I wanted to show you." I unlocked Mary's door and turned on the light, illuminating the scone on the floor. "It looks like she ate part of that sometime today. I thought it was strange that she just left it on the floor."

I watched him perform the same procedures he had done Friday night. Gloves on, photo evidence number cards out, evidence bags ready. He photographed the scone, then picked it up. Before he put it in the bag, he sniffed it.

"What does it smell like?"

"Cherries and almonds."

"Of course. It's one of the scones Becky had brought for yesterday's tea." I watched him seal the bag. "Wait. Isn't cyanide supposed to smell like almonds?"

"Yup. Bitter almonds."

I bit my bottom lip. It looked like Clara was right.

He found the crumpled note under the bed, photographed it, then dropped it into another evidence bag. He continued into the bathroom. I heard the rattle of medicine bottles dropping into evidence bags, and then he came back into the main room.

"What's next?" I asked as Cal took out a Sharpie and started writing on the plastic bags.

"I'll take these into forensics and see if we can find something in any of them that might have caused Mary's symptoms. Then we'll wait for the test results. I need to get these samples to the lab ASAP."

He started for the stairs, then turned back so suddenly that I almost ran into him.

"By the way, where is Paul Peterson? Did he go to the hospital with Mary?"

"I haven't seen him since breakfast."

His eyes narrowed. "Call me as soon as he shows up. I'd like to ask him some questions."

"You can't think he had something to do with this."

"Emma-"

"I know." I suppressed a groan. "Everyone is a

suspect."

"Not only a suspect. Paul might have had a motive for getting rid of Mary." He pulled a toothpick out of his pocket. Before he stuck it in the corner of his mouth, he said, "But there's always the possibility that Mary wasn't the one who was supposed to be poisoned. Maybe Paul was the intended target."

I shuddered. "I hate to think about either of those possibilities."

"Meanwhile, stay safe. I don't like what's going on here. Possible poisoning, missing suspects, intruders, and a murder. All since you came to town."

"You aren't blaming me, are you?"

"No, but you have to admit that it looks pretty suspicious."

"It's only a coincidence."

Cal shifted the duffel in his hand and put his hat on. "There's no such thing as coincidence."

After he left, I made sure the door was latched, then turned around. Clara still stood near the reception desk, her hand in the pocket of her robe.

"Well, that was interesting," she said.

"Interesting? One of our guests might have been poisoned." My throat grew tight as my voice rose. "I'd call that a bit more than interesting."

She smiled that warm, motherly smile again and threaded her arm through my elbow. "I know how to calm those nerves. You need a nice cup of chamomile tea with sugar and plenty of milk."

As she pulled out a chair at the nearest table for me, a heavy metal object in her bathrobe pocket bumped against my knee. I watched this sweet older lady make a cup of tea for each of us, but my mind was whirling. I hugged my elbows. Clara was packing a gun in that fluffy pink robe. No one was who or what they seemed to be, including Clara. Sweet motherly types didn't pack a pistol.

Clara put my cup in front of me, along with the pitcher of milk and the sugar bowl.

"There's nothing like a nice cup of milky tea to end a stressful evening, don't you think?" She spooned sugar into the cup, then stirred the tea as she added milk from the pitcher. "I love to make chamomile like this. It reminds me of the cambric tea my grandmother made for me when I was a child."

I wrapped my chilled fingers around the fragile teacup. "I've never had cambric tea," I heard myself saying, while the other part of my brain wondered how much Clara knew about poisons.

My imagination was working overtime with my brain so tired. I lifted the cup to my nose and breathed in the steamy fragrance.

"Mm. You're right. This is perfectly relaxing." I took a sip then put the cup back in the saucer. "Did you want to go back to your room? I can wait up for the others."

"I wouldn't think of leaving you alone after the evening we've had. We'll stay up and wait for news together."

The inn doors were locked at ten o'clock every night, but the two couples who had gone out to dinner were home before then.

Annie and Roger came in first.

"We're going out early in the morning," Roger said. "We won't be here for breakfast."

"Thanks for letting me know," I said. "Where are you heading?"

"Up to Devils Tower. According to the

guidebook, there are some good trails up there, and you can even climb the tower if you want to."

"Not this time," Annie said with a warning note in her voice. Then she took a step closer to me. "Has Paul come back yet?"

I shook my head. "Not yet."

"I do hope nothing has happened to him."

Roger grabbed her arm and started for the stairs. "He's a big boy. He can take care of himself."

When Sam and Nora came in, they didn't do anything more than call "Good night" as they hurried up the steps.

"It's time for their favorite television show," Clara whispered to me. "That one about the treasure hunters that travel around the world. They watch it every night."

"How do you know that?"

She sat back in her chair. "They leave their windows open and the sound drifts down to my room."

Before I could ask what else she knew about the Nelsons, my phone rang. It was Rose.

"The hospital admitted Mary. She's in fragile shape," she said. "Clara was right. It was poison."

"Do they know what kind?"

I glanced at Clara and put my phone on speaker. Rose's voice carried enough for her to hear.

"Not yet. The lab here will be running tests, but meanwhile they've been able to counteract her symptoms. One thing that will help will be to know how she ingested it. I hope Cal will be able to determine that."

Rose said they would be home soon, and we hung up. Clara and I stared at each other.

"You were right," I said.

"I was afraid I was."

"But who would poison Mary?" I remembered what Cal had said, that perhaps Paul had been the intended target all along. Or perhaps Paul had decided it was time to get rid of Mary.

I drank the rest of my tea. One thing was certain. In the morning, someone needed to start looking for Paul. And that someone was going to be me.

Cal walked into the inn just as I was clearing up after breakfast. The spinach and red pepper frittata had been popular with the guests, even with Mary's illness and Paul's disappearance overshadowing everyone's mood. Baked Brie with rye toast squares had been a great accompaniment to the frittata, and I had been snacking on the leftovers as I worked.

"Hey. What's up?" I asked.

Cal laid his hat on the reception desk and walked over to the buffet counter where the last of the cheese oozed on a warmed marble cutting board.

"I need to seal Mary's room off now that it's a crime scene."

He picked up a piece of toast and asked permission with raised eyebrows. When I nodded, he scooped up a dollop of the Brie with it.

"You think her poisoning was intentional? It wasn't just food poisoning? That cherry scone should have been refrigerated."

He caught my eye with a look that sent a chill through me. "Emma, it wasn't food poisoning."

I swallowed. Hard. "If it was intentional, then that means attempted murder."

"If she survives. If not, then we have another murder case on our hands."

"I'll go up and unlock the door."

After swiping another toast square through the cheese, Cal followed me to the staircase. "Has Paul Peterson shown up yet?"

"No," I said, sorting through my key ring for the master key. "No one has seen him since yesterday morning. Some of the other guests are getting worried." At least Annie was. I had to admit that I was, too. I opened Mary's door.

"We also need to check Paul's room," Cal said, holding out his hand for the key.

I stared at him as a horrifying thought passed through my mind. "You don't think he was poisoned, too, do you?" I swallowed again. My stomach suddenly queasy. "Could he have been here all this time? D-dead?"

Cal's face was grim as he took the key. "Stay here until I tell you it's clear."

He unlocked the door and pushed it open with his fingertips. It was empty.

As he walked in, Cal looked all around. "It doesn't look like he even moved in."

At his nod, I followed him and checked the pass door. It was locked.

"They paid for two rooms, but only used one," I said. "At least one of them wanted to keep up the appearance that they were staying in separate rooms."

"That doesn't sound like the Hollywood type."

"It sounds like Mary. I don't think she wanted anyone to suspect they anything other than a professional relationship."

"You observed them together quite a bit. Do you think Paul could be capable of murder?"

"You mean Dead Dick?"

"Or Mary."

I considered Pretentious Paul. He was arrogant, self-centered, and a ham. But a murderer?

"I think it's more likely that he would just fire Mary and cast her aside rather than kill her. A murder would ruin his career if anyone found out, wouldn't it?"

"Or maybe in his twisted sense of values, he thought the possibility of a murder or two connected to him would bring more viewers to his show."

I followed Cal out of the room and watched him take a roll of crime scene tape out of his duffel.

"How could he keep doing his show if he's in prison for murder?"

"Killers never figure they'll be caught."

As Cal stretched the tape across the two doorways, I considered where Paul could be.

"Since Paul said he was going up to the mine yesterday, don't you think we should start looking for him there?"

Cal stretched the paper booties over his shoes. "He might have been there yesterday at some point, but he'll be long gone now. I wouldn't be surprised to find evidence that Paul poisoned Mary and then took off. He'd want to put as much distance between himself and the crime scene as possible."

"But what if he didn't poison her? What if the poison had been meant for him?" Someone needed to remind the deputy that we were working with more than one theory.

"Then the evidence will tell us." He snapped on his latex gloves, infuriatingly calm. "So let me process the scene. Don't you have work to do?"

He ducked under the crime scene tape, ignoring me. I went back downstairs to finish clearing up from breakfast, getting more irritated at Cal with every minute. He seemed set on treating Paul as a suspect while I had the feeling he might be another victim. But how could I convince him I was right?

The mine was the key, but I had never been there. I wasn't even sure how to find it. I texted Becky to see if she was available to help and she answered almost immediately.

Wear hiking boots and meet me outside in ten.

I was on the front porch in five minutes and settled down on one of the chairs to watch for Becky. Where could Paul be? Had something happened to him at the mine? Was he hurt or...worse?

I couldn't let my mind go there. Pretentious Paul. Everything about him said "look at me." Even his signature red scarf. It wasn't like him to stay out of the public eye for long.

With that thought, I took my phone from my pocket and opened my social media app. I searched for Paul's name.

Just then, Becky came jogging up the driveway. She joined me on the porch.

"What are you doing?" She stood next to my chair and looked at my screen.

"I thought if Paul could, he would be posting on social media. He puts up something new three or four times a day." I scrolled through his page. "Nothing since yesterday morning."

I tapped the picture to enlarge it. Paul had taken a

video of himself at the entrance to Graves' Folly mine. I turned up the volume.

"Here we are at the entrance to this mine in the Black Hills, reported to be haunted by the ghosts of the three men who were trapped inside during a mining accident more than one hundred years ago." The video panned from his face to the dark entrance of the mine. "My assistant and I will be setting up our patented ghost-chasing instruments in this very mine tonight, and we'll bring you all the excitement on the next episode of Ghost Chasers. Don't miss it!"

The video panned back to Paul again as he struck the "Ghost Chaser" pose, then it ended.

"When did he post that?" Becky asked.

I looked at the time on the entry. "It was just after ten o'clock yesterday morning."

"And nothing since then?"

I went through a few other social media sites, but the most recent thing Paul had posted was that same video.

"He said that he and Mary would be in the mine last night, but he didn't know she would be in the hospital."

"He planned on being there," Becky said. "We know why Mary wasn't there, but where was Paul? You wanted to go up to the mine to look for him?"

"Let's go."

We walked up Graves' Gulch Road, a gravel road that went up a steep grade deep into the forest. After about a quarter mile, we reached an open gate with a forest service sign next to it.

Becky motioned to our left. "There's the trail to the mine."

"So, everything from this gate on is part of the

National Forest?"

"That's right. This fence marks the boundary."

"It's cool that Rose owns a gold mine," I said as I followed her along the trail.

"It isn't much of a gold mine. My family says it's bad luck."

"You don't believe that do you?"

"Not really." Her tone of voice confirmed that she really hadn't thought much about it. "But Gran sure was happy to sell the property to Rose when she wanted to buy it."

"Had it been for sale very long?"

"It was never on the market. Rose just approached Gran and the deed was done." Becky stopped. "Here's the entrance."

We had left the boundary fence on our right as we walked. The trail had climbed up the side of a hill until we came to a cliff face. The mine opening was in front of us, and the cliff towered thirty feet or so above.

"This is where Paul filmed that video we watched." I pulled out my phone, intending to watch it again to double-check.

"Don't bother with your phone. There's no cell service here."

I stared at Becky. "What kind of place doesn't have cell service?"

"The wilderness." She grinned. "There's a spot farther along the trail, kind of an overlook, and you can pick up a signal there."

"But we get great reception at the inn."

"Rose has cable internet and Wi-Fi at the inn. This is the forest."

I gestured toward the dark opening in front of us.

"Should we see if Paul is inside?"

The floor was dry, solid, smooth rock except for an old set of rails going down the center of the tunnel. The roof started low, then rose to a height of about ten feet once we were inside. Becky and I both turned on our cell phone flashlights. The tunnel went on in front of us, sloping downward and to the left.

"I haven't been in here since I was a kid," Becky said, shining her light on the walls next to us. "There." She pointed to a gleaming hair-thin thread in the rock. "That's the folly, as Gran says. Great-great-grandpa followed these threads deep into the mountain, but he never found the lode."

"You mean that's the gold?"

"That's it. When we were kids, we used to try to dig out bits of it with our pocketknives."

"Did you ever get much?"

"Never. I heard that Grandpa always said there was a big lode just beyond the next layer of rock, but mining is a hard job. It took him most of his life to dig out this much, and that was with hiring drillers and blasting."

"Is that why he named it Graves' Folly?"

"He never called it that. I heard he got a little crazy toward the end, but he insisted the gold was there until his dying day."

"But some men died in a cave-in? Or is that just one of Paul's ghost stories?"

"The cave-in was real. Three of the miners died. Grandpa made it out, along with the rest of the crew. But that was the end of the digging."

I looked down the passage that disappeared into darkness beyond the flashlight's range.

"Did they ever recover the bodies?"

"Nope. This is their tomb until the end of time."

I shuddered. "I don't see any sign that Paul is here, but we need to go as far as we can, don't you think?"

"It isn't much farther to the cave-in." She crossed to the other side of the tunnel. "I have to show you this." Thousands of sparkles reflected in her flashlight's glow. "I call this the fairy wall. Cal and the other boys always laughed at me, but this is my favorite part of the mine. I used to pretend that this was the opening to the fairy realm."

"It's beautiful." It was, but my mind was on the darkness around us, not fairies. "Let's keep going."

The tunnel led us on for several more yards, continuing a gentle slope downward. Then our lights illuminated a pile of rocks.

"This is the end," Becky said. "According to Grandpa's map, the tunnel extends a few hundred yards beyond the cave-in, and that's where the shafts go down. Grandpa followed those gold threads until his luck ran out with the cave-in."

I shuddered again, thinking of the three men who had been trapped behind that wall of rock, or perhaps crushed by it.

Becky must have felt it, too. "Let's get out of here."

We walked back up the tunnel. Soon we could see the light filtering in from the entrance, and then we were free. I looked back into the dark hole. If there were such things as ghosts, that would be where you would find them.

"What next?" Becky asked. "We know Paul was here because he made that video. But where did he go after this?"

"No one saw him return to the inn, but he must

have gone somewhere to post the video on the internet."

"Maybe he went to the overlook. It isn't far away."

Becky took off at a brisk walk, continuing along the trail we had followed to the mine. We climbed up, then through a narrow fissure between some rocks, until we came out on top of the cliff.

"The overlook is this way."

Becky led the way along the narrow path around an outcropping of rocks, and then we were on a wide ledge. Below us was the most beautiful canyon I had ever seen.

"Wow." I looked down into the canyon, but the bottom was obscured by thick pine trees. Across the canyon was another line of rimrock, outlining the opposite side. A large bird was flying at the same level where we were standing. "Is that an eagle?" I pointed toward it.

"Not an eagle. A vulture." Becky pointed above us where three more birds circled over the canyon. "See? There are some more. There must be something dead at the bottom." She pulled out her cell phone. "Do you have any reception here?"

I had three bars. I went closer to the edge of the overlook, and it increased to four.

"It's enough for Paul to post his video. He could have done it here."

"Watch your step," Becky said. "You're getting close to the edge."

I looked down at my feet. She was right. My toes were too close for comfort. As I took a step back, I noticed a bright red thread caught on a bush. I took a picture of it.

"Look at this." I held the thread up for Becky to

see. "Could this be from Paul's scarf?"

She took it from me and looked closely. "It's the same color. So, maybe. But where is he now?"

Both of us turned toward the cliff's edge. I didn't want to look over it, but I had to rule out the possibility.

I fought the queasy feeling in my stomach and inched back to the edge of the cliff. When I got too close and felt vertigo taking over, I dropped to my knees, then lay on my stomach. I scooted forward until my head cleared the edge of the rock face. Beneath the overlook the cliff cut back, then met the ground in a precipitous free fall to the canyon's bottom.

Far below, wedged between rocks as big as Rose's Range Rover, was Paul's bright red scarf, glowing like a scarlet bird against the gray granite background. I shut my eyes, but I had already seen the rest. The scarf wreathed Paul's face. His expression was frozen in contorted panic, staring sightless into the sky.

Nine

By the time Paul's body had been recovered and sent to the coroner's office, afternoon teatime had come and gone. No one noticed. Cal had asked the guests and staff, including Becky, to meet him in the dining room and we waited in silence, except for an occasional sniff from Annie. Roger sat next to her, frowning as he stared at the floor.

Just as Cal walked in the front door, Wil came in from the direction of the kitchen and took a seat at an empty table.

"Good, you're all here," Cal said. He set his duffel bag on the nearest table, the one where Roger and Annie were sitting, and laid his hat on top. He took a notepad from his shirt pocket.

As he flipped it open, Roger said, "Was he murdered?"

"From my preliminary examination, it looks like Paul Peterson's death was an accident. He stepped too close to the edge of the cliff and fell."

From my vantage point at the edge of the group of tables, I could see most of the guests' reactions. Roger put his arm around Annie's shoulders, while Nora dabbed at her mascaraed eyes with a napkin. Sam leaned his arms on his knees and stared at his laced fingers. Wil was the only one who didn't look moved by the news. Probably thinking about tomorrow's breakfast menu, I thought.

"I'll answer any questions I can," Cal said.

"What about his television show?" Roger asked. "Will it be canceled?"

"I can't answer that one. You would have to contact the production company or someone."

"Did he..." Tears trickled down Annie's cheeks. "Did he suffer?"

"It looks like his death was instantaneous, so no. I don't think so."

Sam slapped his hand on the table. "Since it was an accident, we're free to go on with our plans, aren't we?"

Nora punched his shoulder. "Shut up. A man is dead and all you can think about is going to another casino."

He scowled at her. "Face it. No one is going to spend a lot of time grieving over Paul Peterson."

Annie buried her face in her hands as Roger rose to his feet and faced Sam, his fists clenched.

"Not everyone is as heartless as you." His voice quavered. "Some of us actually liked the man and we're sorry he's dead."

Rose raised her hand, bringing Cal's attention to her. "I think what Mr. Nelson is trying to ask is that if the death was an accident, we aren't restrained from going about our normal lives."

"That's right." Cal flipped his notebook closed and put on his hat. "We still have the matter of Dick Brill's murder to investigate, but you may all carry on as usual."

The group was silent as Cal picked up his duffel and headed for the door. I followed him out the front door and caught up with him just as he reached his police SUV.

"What makes you so sure it was an accident? You have to admit that it looks very suspicious for Paul to die like that just after Mary was poisoned."

He leaned against the side of the SUV and crossed his arms. "You think so? Maybe it was just a coincidence."

"I thought you didn't believe in coincidences."

"I don't. But I don't think you'll like my theory."

I leaned against the SUV next to him. "Try me."

"Paul poisoned Mary, then went up to the mine to record his social media posts."

"Why would he do that?"

"To throw suspicion off of himself if we figured out the poisoning was intentional."

I had to admit that it sounded plausible so far. "Go on."

"But when he went to the overlook to post his video, he got too close to the edge and slipped off."

"I can see how that would happen." I remembered the vertigo I had felt on the overlook. "But then we're talking about coincidence again."

"Emma, there is no evidence that his death was anything but an accident. But the forensics team is up at the overlook combing the area, and we won't have the coroner's report for a day or so."

"There's still a chance that it's murder?"

"Don't be so eager. Do you really want to have another murder case on our hands? Besides, there is nothing to connect Paul Peterson to Dick Brill, is there?"

No, I didn't want another murder connected with the inn, but I had a gut feeling it was.

"It could be random," I said. "Maybe the murderer only kills when he sees a good opportunity."

"Murders are rarely random." He took a toothpick out of his shirt pocket and held it between his fingers while he talked. "There are very few people who kill just to kill. There has to be a reason."

"A motive," I thought, remembering all the Agatha Christie stories I had read and television mystery shows I had watched.

"I saw you watching the others in there." Cal nodded his head toward the inn. "What do you think of how they received the news?"

"I think everyone reacted the way I thought they would. A few tears, but mostly somber."

"Did you notice that Wil didn't show any reaction?"

"Yes, I did. But I'm beginning to expect that sort of thing from him. He's pretty self-centered."

Cal nodded in agreement. "And speaking of murder, have you come up with any ideas about Dick Brill's death?"

"No progress at all. He seems to have been well-liked by everyone who knew him, and I can't find any reason why someone would kill him."

"Maybe he was just in the wrong place at the wrong time."

"I thought you said that there has to be a motive for murder?"

"Seeing too much can be the strongest motive of all." Cal stuck the toothpick in his mouth.

"The wrong place at the wrong time describes

poor Dick. My suite was definitely the wrong place." I leaned back against Cal's SUV and gazed at the town of Paragon below us. Something tickled at the back of my mind.

"I need to get going. Forensics will be on site for several more hours, so try to keep folks away from the spot if you can."

"Hmm?" That tickle had distracted me. "Oh, sure. We'll stay away." I shuddered. I didn't think I'd want to go into the forest again. Ever. I started toward the front door.

"Hey," Cal said. I turned around. "We're still having supper together on Saturday, right?"

I grinned at the anxious look on his face. "Sure thing. Saturday."

"Do me a favor and don't say anything to Becky, okay?"

"Are you afraid she'll tease you?"

He grimaced. "She wouldn't leave me alone until she pumped me for every detail. She's worse than a little sister."

Cal drove off, mostly to avoid my grin, I thought.

"Who's worse than a little sister?"

Becky was standing on the front porch, leaning over the rail.

"How much of that conversation did you hear?"

"Enough to find out that Cal is keeping something from me. What is it?"

I joined her on the porch. "I can't tell you."

She slumped down on one of the rockers. "Some friend you are."

"Okay, I'll tell you all about it, but not yet."

"I guess I'll have to be happy with that."

She set the rocker in motion.

"It's no use." The rocking chair stopped. "I can't stand not knowing. Can you at least give me a hint?"

"Cal was right. He said you wouldn't leave it alone."

"At least tell me what the two of you were talking about out here in the driveway."

"We were talking about Dick Brill's murder." There was that something in the back of my mind again. What was it about Dick's murder that I was missing?

"Was that all?"

"He wants everyone to stay away from the scene until the forensic team finishes investigating."

"No problem there," She got up and started walking toward the driveway. "That's the wrong place to be right now."

That was it. The tickle. I waved goodbye to Becky and sat in the rocker. What had Cal said? That Dick might have been in the wrong place at the wrong time?

I went through the details in my head. Both the rose quartz – the murder weapon – and the bits of lichen Cal had found meant that Dick must have been murdered somewhere in the forest, not in my suite. And then Paul met his end in the forest, too. It was tenuous, but it was a link between the two deaths.

But what did it mean? Was Paul murdered by the same person who had killed Dick? And why?

I groaned. One possible answer led me right back to the same question. What was the motive?

It had to have something to do with the forest. Trees? Rocks? More trees? What was there that might be worth killing someone? I looked up at Grizzly Peak and shivered. In the slanted rays of the evening sun, I could imagine anything lurking in those trees.

I shivered again. The air was taking on a chill. As I went inside the inn, I met Roger and Annie going out to dinner. Sam and Nora followed them. Rose, Clara, and Montgomery were still sitting in the dining room. Wil had left, probably gone upstairs to his apartment. I stifled a yawn. I didn't blame him. After today's events, I was ready for a good long sleep after I warmed up a can of soup in my kitchenette.

Before I went to my own suite, I straightened the reception desk. It was a catch-all for every stray object. Today it was the lens cap to a camera. I put it in the lost and found basket, then noticed an envelope in the mail basket. It had no address, only Rose's name, typewritten like the other notes.

I picked it up and glanced at the back. The envelope wasn't sealed, but the flap was tucked in. Rose and her friends looked relaxed, like they weren't worried about Paul's death, or Mary's poisoning, or the dead body in my room that had started all of this. Did I really want to disturb them?

The typed name on the front of the letter seemed to mock me. I couldn't keep this from Rose. She had to know about it.

Montgomery was facing me and stood when he saw what I had in my hand as I approached the trio. Rose turned to me, her face paling when she saw the envelope. She pressed her lips together.

"Another one." Montgomery's voice was hard, like steel. "We need to call the deputy in on this."

"But he just left," I said, my tired brain protesting the idea of talking to anyone tonight. I just wanted to sleep.

"Then we can catch him before he gets too far

away," Rose said.

I dropped the envelope on the table and my stomach twisted. Why hadn't I left the envelope in Rose's mailbox until morning?

Montgomery's phone call had pulled Cal away from his supper, which put him in a growly mood.

"This envelope was in Rose's in-box?" he asked.

"I found it after you left," I said.

I sat next to Clara as he examined the envelope.

"Have you opened this?" he asked Rose.

"No. I can tell it's another threatening note, and I suspect it was sent by the same person as the other ones."

"The other ones? Why haven't I heard about these before now?"

Montgomery and Rose exchanged glances, and Rose brought out the other four notes from her sweater pocket. She laid them on the table. Five matching envelopes. The only difference was in the way they were addressed.

"As you can see, I started receiving these while I was still in Arizona for the winter. Montgomery and I thought they were connected to the memoir I'm in the process of writing."

Cal slipped gloves on and opened the first note Rose handed him. He read it out loud. "Hello. You didn't think I'd find you? Think again." Then he opened the second. "Roses are red. Violets are blue. A Rose isn't dead. And neither are you. Yet."

Rose's smile was grim. "The note writer isn't a

very good poet."

The deputy went on to the third one. "Don't return to the Sweetbrier Inn if you value your life." He laid it on the table next to the others. "This is a death threat. Why didn't you contact the authorities?"

"I did." Rose laid a hand on Montgomery's arm. "Up until recently, I still thought the notes pertained to my memoirs. When I received this one, I called my friend Montgomery. He's retired now, but when we worked together, he looked after our security."

"I thought you said you contacted the authorities."

Montgomery took a business card out of his pocket. It was the same one he had shown me earlier.

Cal read it. "The WIO? What's that?"

"The World Intelligence Organization."

"Never heard of it."

Montgomery leaned back in his chair. "You aren't meant to."

The deputy studied the older man as if he was sizing him up.

"What did you do to investigate this after Rose called you?"

"I put an alert out on all of Rose's known enemies and accompanied her home when she left Arizona."

Rose had known enemies? There was a lot I still didn't know about my aunt.

"You're her bodyguard?"

"You could call it that."

Rose handed the fourth envelope to Cal, the one that had appeared the day before.

He opened it and read, "I have warned you. Get out before someone else dies."

Cal fished in his shirt pocket and pulled out a toothpick. "It looks like someone is trying to get you to leave the inn."

"That is what has us baffled," Montgomery said. "The warnings seem to be connected to Rose and the Sweetbrier, but we can't figure out why."

"You said Rose has known enemies?" Cal stuck the toothpick into the left corner of his mouth.

"From my days with WIO," Rose said. "But none of them have come to the surface."

"It appears that most of them are out of circulation," Montgomery said.

"In prison?" Cal picked up today's envelope.

"Or eliminated." Montgomery's face was impassive.

Cal slid the note from the envelope, looked at it, then read it aloud. "You didn't heed my warning. Now Paul Peterson is dead. More will follow."

He laid it on the table.

"Then Paul's death wasn't an accident," I said. I clenched my hands together in my lap to keep them from trembling as a cold chill ran through me. Someone had killed Paul, poisoned Mary, and murdered Dick. The incidents must be connected, but how?

"It could be that the note writer took advantage of the situation to scare Rose." Cal leaned on the table. He looked as weary as I felt.

"Well, it isn't working." Rose sat straight in her chair, her shoulders squared and her chin up. "I've faced worse threats than this and never backed down."

"But there are others at risk this time, dear."

The voice was Clara's. She had been sitting between Rose and me, quietly observing.

Rose nodded and grasped her friend's hand.

"You're right. I couldn't live with myself if you or anyone else at the inn was hurt." She looked at Cal. "What do we need to do to find this person? Through legal means, of course."

Her comment made me wonder what illegal means she was familiar with.

"First, we need to find out who wrote these notes," Cal said. He lined the notes up on the table in order. "They have all been printed on a typewriter, not a computer printer."

"How can you tell that?" I asked, leaning in to see the printing better.

"First of all," he said, turning one of the notes over. "You can see the typewriter impression on the back of the paper. Printers don't leave those marks. There is also this." He pointed to the capital R in two of the notes and on the envelopes. "See how the curve of the R is smudged? That tells me that the note writer used the same typewriter to type all four notes and the envelopes."

"It's like a fingerprint," said Montgomery. "It will help identify the typewriter if we find it."

"When we find it," said Cal. "This last note didn't come through the mail. It was probably placed in Rose's in-box by someone here at the inn."

"You mean that the murderer is one of us?" My voice trembled and I took a breath. "How can that be?"

"I'll have to do a search of the inn." Cal's toothpick shifted to the other side of his mouth. "With your permission, I'll search all your rooms. After the guests return, I'll search theirs."

"Don't you need a warrant?" I asked.

"Not if I have permission." He looked at each of

us in turn, waiting for our assent. All three of us agreed.

"Start with my suite," Rose said. "I'll unlock my office door for you."

"The rest of you stay here," Cal said, looking directly at me. "Don't leave this room."

I nodded and he followed Rose into her rooms.

Rose joined us again and we sat, looking at each other.

"Do you think he'll find what he's looking for?" asked Clara.

"If it is in the inn, he'll find it." Montgomery stretched, then went over to the tea service counter. "Can I bring anyone some tea? Or something stronger?"

"Some herbal tea will be fine," Rose said.

We waited. After what seemed like an hour, Cal came out of Rose's suite and went to Clara's room. I checked the clock. It had only been fifteen minutes.

Then Wil came down the stairs. "What's up?"

Rose filled him in. "Cal will want to search your room, too," she said. "But he'll need your permission."

Wil shrugged. "I don't have a problem with that."

We all watched Cal come out of Clara's room and head upstairs. He didn't make a comment.

I finished my cup of tea and looked at my watch. It was after eight and my stomach was letting me know I hadn't had anything for supper yet.

Cal came back downstairs and stopped on the bottom step.

"Emma, I need you to come with me."

I went to join him, followed by the rest of the crew. Cal stopped them.

"Only Emma. I need the rest of you to remain here."

As I followed him up the stairs, I asked, "What did you find?"

He didn't answer but led the way into my suite. The door to the coat closet in the corner next to the kitchenette was standing open. He pointed at the items he had put on my kitchen counter.

"Can you explain those?"

A typewriter and a box with stationery filled the tiny space.

"Where did they come from?"

"You need to tell me. I found them on the top shelf in your closet."

"They aren't mine. I haven't used that closet since I arrived last week."

Cal leaned against the counter. "I thought that might be the case. It was empty except for these items." The toothpick switched sides. "It looks like someone is still trying to frame you."

"You believe me?"

"From what Wil told me, you only had one suitcase when you arrived at the inn, plus the cat and his supplies. You didn't bring the typewriter with you."

"Someone put it in my room to make it look like I had been the one to write the notes?"

"It was probably the same person who put Dick Brill's body in here. If I was a different kind of investigator, I might have overlooked the inconsistencies and tagged you as my prime suspect."

"What do we do now?"

Cal ran one hand through his curly hair. "I want to put the real murderer off his guard. I'll let the others know that I have some leads, but not enough evidence to pinpoint a suspect."

"I get it. You think the bad guy will get careless as he tries to provide more evidence to make me seem guilty."

"He or she. It could be anyone."

"You must have some idea."

"I have a few theories, but I could be wrong. I can't share them with you because it might prejudice you in your observations."

"Observations?"

"You still want to help in the investigation, right?"

I nodded.

"I need you to be my eyes and ears here at the inn. People will talk more freely when there isn't a police officer hanging around."

A shudder ran through me. "Are you sure it couldn't be someone outside the inn? Someone who has found a way to sneak in and plant these things?"

"Without anyone seeing them? I think it's unlikely."

I thought of the people at the inn, all of whom had become part of my life in the past week since I had arrived. Could one of them really be a murderer?

Cal studied my face, his rich brown eyes reassuring and comforting.

"You will need to be very careful. Our murderer is clever, and if he thinks he's lost the game he might decide to get rid of you, too."

My mouth was dry. "This isn't a game."

"Not to us. But to the person who is doing this, it's like a game of chess. He thinks he's in control of the board, but we need to take that control out of his hands."

Cal's radio beeped. He grabbed it from his belt and walked into the kitchen where he spoke briefly in quiet tones. He came back to the living room and stood in front of me, his face stern.

"What is it?"

His answer was gruff. "Mary has passed away. We have three murders on our hands."

"Did they find out what poisoned her?"

"The final tests proved it was arsenic that had been laced in the scone she ate." Cal ran one hand through his curls again. "Keep this news quiet until tomorrow morning. I want to be the one to announce it to the group. When will they all be together?"

"At breakfast. Everyone is in the dining room by seven, even if they have plans to go somewhere."

Cal nodded. "I'd appreciate it if you stay in your suite for the rest of the evening." He gathered up the typewriter and stationery. "I'll let Rose and the others know that I found these things in your room and let them draw their own conclusions. I'll be back in the morning. Meanwhile, I'll examine those notes for fingerprints. Maybe he got careless."

He closed the door on his way out. I turned the deadbolt behind him then stared at the lock. The murderer had let himself into my room at least twice. No lock seemed to keep him out. I pulled the ottoman over and pushed it against the door. It might not keep a murderer out, but at least he wouldn't take me by surprise.

I dropped onto the sectional. My body was exhausted, but my mind was racing. Poor Mary. And poor Paul. Who could have killed them? Why? And how were their deaths connected to Dick Brill?

Tim jumped onto the back of the couch and

climbed down into my lap. I stroked his sleek black fur, then scratched his chin as he shut his eyes and purred.

My first move after breakfast was to find the arsenic.

Ten

I was up before dawn on Friday morning even though I had not slept well. But as early as it was, Wil had still arrived in the kitchen before me.

Grabbing my cup of coffee, I leaned on the counter and watched while Wil made pancakes.

"Won't those pancakes be cold by the time we serve them to the guests?"

Wil smiled at me, then winked. "If I was making pancakes, then yes, they would be."

What had put him in such a good mood this morning? I took another sip of my coffee, closing my eyes as the rich brew slid down my throat. I needed this.

"Okay, wise guy. If those aren't pancakes, then they must be crepes."

He poured a ladle of batter into the pan and swirled it with a practiced move. "That's right. I'm making crepe cups filled with a prosciutto, egg and cheese."

"Sounds good." I took another sip of coffee, remembering Cal's assignment. "Where did you learn to cook so well?"

"I went to culinary school in Paris," he said, sliding the finished crepe onto a cooling rack and ladling more batter into the pan. "One thing I learned there is that cooking techniques can be taught, but true talent is something a chef is born with. You either have it or you don't."

"How long did you live in Paris?"

"I took a one-year program at École Pierre Cordon after I graduated from the New York Institute."

"I love Paris." I leaned on the counter, my coffee mug snug between my hands. "Did you ever go to Chez Riennes on the Left Bank? Don't you love their croissants?"

He paused to flip the crepe in the pan with an impressive move. "My schooling kept me busy. I didn't get to tour the city much."

"That's too bad." I finished my coffee and poured myself another one, trying to hide my surprise. Chez Riennes was known as a hangout for the students from École Pierre Cordon. "It was worth all your work, though. After all, you landed this job."

"You forget that I'm not an employee at the inn. I'm a part owner." He slid the last crepe onto the cooling rack.

"That's right. I remember Rose mentioning it." I turned my mug in my hands. "That's impressive for someone your age, isn't it? I mean, don't most chefs have to establish a reputation before they own their own place?"

"The inheritance I received from my father helped."

"Oh, Wil, I'm sorry. I didn't know you had lost your father."

He reached under the counter for a muffin pan. "It isn't a big deal."

"How old were you when he passed away?"

"I was eighteen and on my own." He pushed the crepes into the oversized muffin cups.

"My father passed away a few years ago. I still miss him, even though I left home when I was twenty."

Wil shrugged and kept working.

"You used the inheritance to pay for your schooling?"

"Yes." He glanced at me. "Why all the questions?"

It was my turn to shrug. "Just curious. We've been working together for a week, and I realized I still don't know you well."

"Why bother?" Wil took a carton of eggs from the cooler. "It isn't like you're going to be here much longer."

Just then Becky walked into the kitchen with her daily delivery of baked items. "Who's leaving?"

"Emma is, if Deputy Cal can make the charges stick."

"What?" Becky dropped the box on the counter. "What did I miss?"

"Just Emma's imminent arrest." Wil grinned at her. "Some key evidence was found in her closet."

"Arrest? Evidence?" Becky turned to me, her hands on her hips. "Emma, what's going on?"

"I'll tell you later." I glanced at Wil, but he had turned his back to us. "Come on. You can help me get the dining room ready for breakfast."

"I can't this morning. I have to get back to the café."

I linked elbows with her. "Then I'll walk you to your car."

We left the kitchen and went out on the front porch. The sun was just coming up and the birds were singing. It looked like it was going to be a beautiful day.

Becky stopped on the porch and faced me. "What's going on? What was Wil talking about?"

"It's all right. Cal found the typewriter in my suite."

"What typewriter?"

I filled her in on what had happened the evening before, including the news of Mary's death.

"And Wil thinks you're the suspect because Cal found the typewriter in your room? Anyone could have put it there."

"That's just the point." I motioned for her to keep her voice quiet. "Only people who know the inn and have access to it could have planted that evidence. And yes, Cal knows it was planted."

"So, the bad guy has to be someone in the inn?"

"Or someone who comes here frequently."

Becky's face grew stony. "Like me."

I laughed. "I know you better than that." I gave her a hug. "You have never been a suspect to me."

She grinned. "Thanks. But poor Mary. Why would someone murder her?"

"That's the hard part. I can't see how the three murders are connected. Dick was killed before Mary and Paul got here."

"If we knew why they were killed, that would lead us to the culprit, wouldn't it?"

"It would sure help."

"I'll keep my eyes and ears open. Gran needs me to work in the café today waiting tables. I'll let you know if I hear anything juicy."

"Thanks."

As Becky drove away, I went back into the inn. Cal arrived right at seven o'clock, and all four of our guests were in the dining room, along with Rose, Clara, and Montgomery. Mysterious Monty and Cunning Clara. What a pair. I was glad they were such loyal friends for Rose.

Cal caught my eye then cocked his head toward the door. I got the message. He didn't want me hanging around while he told the guests what he had found. I went out the front door, then headed around the building to the garage's side door. I had decided last night that this would be the perfect opportunity to start searching for the arsenic.

I walked through the garage to the greenhouse. With the morning sun shining through the glass roof, the place was as warm and humid as a summer day in Chicago.

Wil kept his gardening supplies in a plastic storage cupboard to the right of the door. I had expected something like an old garden shed, but Wil's cupboard was as clean and neat as his kitchen. Every spot was labeled. A trowel. A fork. A hand rake. Fertilizers. And yes, pesticides. I looked at the labels on the packages one by one, reading every ingredient. No arsenic.

I crossed over to Rose's side of the greenhouse. She kept her supplies in a cupboard that matched Wil's, but hers was a jumble. I poked gingerly among the things. Stray bits of string and cotton wool made me think that a mouse had a nest somewhere in there. On the third shelf I found a dirty manila envelope. It was the size of an index card with a typed label stuck on it.

The label contained one word: ARSENIC. I peer at it more closely. The curve of the R was smudged. I put it back and closed the cupboard door with shaking hands. Not Rose. I stepped away from the cupboard. The murderer couldn't be my sweet aunt. Then I remembered Montgomery's cryptic comment the night before, something about Rose's enemies being eliminated.

Was Rose a murderer?

I shook my head, even though I knew it was possible.

I made my way out of the greenhouse and back to the front porch, hoping to catch Cal before he left, but his SUV was no longer in the driveway. I had to talk to someone about my suspicions.

Becky.

I ran down the driveway and headed for the café. The bell above the door tinkled as I went in, right in the middle of the breakfast rush. The small dining room was packed with both locals and tourists. I waved to Gran through the pass-through window from the kitchen as Becky whirled past me.

"I'm glad you're here," she said. "Come in the back and I'll get you an apron. You know how to be a waitress, right?"

I followed her into a back hallway. "Where are the usual workers?"

"The twins, Angie and Allie are both sick with the flu or something. Gran knew Allie wasn't going to come in, so she asked me, but then Angie called in at the last minute. It's been a zoo!" She grinned as she flung an apron toward me. "But you can help for a while, can't you? The rush will be over by eight o'clock, and then I can call one of the other cousins."

I pulled the apron over my head and tied it in back. "I need to talk to you, but I'll help out for a half-hour." I was in no hurry to get back to the inn where I would have to face Rose and everyone else.

It had been years since I had waited tables, but the café menu was simple. I took orders and delivered food until my feet and back were sore from the work, and the tables still filled up as soon as they were vacated. Becky took care of half the tables and acted as cashier, and Gran kept the griddle busy. She was a working fiend the way she had orders out almost as quickly as we turned them in.

Finally, the tables stayed empty. The last customer was Charlie, the minister of the church.

"Okay, now I can talk," Becky said as she wiped down the last empty table. "Charlie and Gran will sit and visit for an hour."

"You can walk me back to the inn." I dropped my apron in the clothes hamper. "Something has come up and I have to talk to someone about it."

We stepped out into the sunny spring morning.

"Isn't this beautiful?" Becky stretched her arms out and turned toward the sun. "I never get tired of days like today."

"I wish I could enjoy it." I crossed my arms and led the way back to the inn.

Becky caught up with me at the corner of Graves' Gulch Road. "Tell me what's bothering you."

"I found the arsenic."

"Great. You've called Cal, haven't you?"

"Not yet. There's a problem." I turned to face her. "I found it in Rose's gardening cupboard in the greenhouse."

"You don't think Rose is the murderer, do you?

She couldn't be."

I couldn't look at her.

"Emma, Rose isn't the murderer."

Becky sounded so sure, but she didn't know about Rose's past. "I don't know. The evidence is pretty strong."

My friend grabbed my elbow and spun me around. "And the evidence against you is strong, too. But you aren't a suspect."

I gave her a quick hug. "Thanks for the reminder. You're right. That envelope could have been planted in Rose's cupboard just like the typewriter was planted in my closet. The real murderer is working hard to throw suspicion on us."

"That means you must be getting close. Isn't that the way it always happens in mystery stories? Once the detective starts getting close to the truth, the bad guy starts panicking?"

"This isn't a mystery story. This is real life."

"And we're dealing with a real murderer." Becky's normal exuberance deflated. "You need to tell Cal what you found."

"And we both need to get back to work." I gave her a smile that I hoped was more hopeful than I felt. "Thanks for being my sounding board."

"Thanks for pitching in at the café." She gave me a return smile. "I need to get back and call someone to help with the lunch crowd. Let me know what Cal says, okay?"

"Sure thing."

As I walked up the hill to the inn, my thoughts went to Rose again. Becky was so sure of her innocence, but was she right? Or maybe the murderer wasn't Rose, but someone close to her. Like Clara. Or

Montgomery. Either one of Rose's loyal friends might kill for her.

And just like that, the suspect list was crowded again.

I had to figure out what the motive for the killings was, and I needed to do it quickly before someone else died.

The main floor of the inn was empty when I got back. I ran up the stairs to my suite to call Cal since I couldn't risk being overheard, but his phone went straight to voicemail.

"Hey, Cal." I paused. This news wasn't something I could leave on a recording. "Give me a call as soon as you get a chance. Thanks."

I closed out of the call and went over to say hello to Tim, who was lying in the sunshine on the back of my sectional. When I realized I was standing in the same spot where I had found Dick, I scooped up the cat. I needed some fresh air.

For the first time all week, the weather was pleasant enough to go out onto my balcony. I sat on one of the two rocking patio chairs with Tim in my lap, lifting my face up to the morning sunshine. Heavenly. Tim purred his agreement. A gentle breeze whispered in the pines towering above the inn, and I settled back in my chair while I scratched the cat's furry chin.

If it hadn't been for Dick's murder and the subsequent deaths, I couldn't imagine a more peaceful spot. But now the possibility of Rose's involvement buzzed around in my mind like a pesky fly. How well did I really know her?

The sound of a door opening drifted up from below, followed by Rose's voice.

"Let's sit out here. It's a beautiful day."

"It's right bonny." It was Clara, following Rose out onto the deck just below me. "I could soak in this sunshine all day."

I heard the scrape of chairs against wood as the two women adjusted their seats.

"How are you doing?" Rose's voice sounded concerned. "This hasn't been a very restful holiday for you."

"I wasn't expecting a holiday, not once I received Monty's telegram. You have him very worried, you know."

Realizing I was eavesdropping, I measured the space between my chair and the door by sight. Could I make it inside without revealing I was here? Or should I stay put? Rose's next comment kept me in my seat.

"Dear Monty. I hope he hasn't done anything foolish for my sake."

"You know he would do anything for you, Rose. Ever since Harry died, he has felt responsible for you."

Rose sighed. "I keep telling him it wasn't his fault. Harry was targeted and there wasn't anything any of us could have done."

The two women were silent. What had Clara meant? Did she think Montgomery would commit murder for Rose? And then try to frame me?

Clara spoke again. "These murders are destroying the inn's reputation, aren't they?"

"You know about the canceled reservations?"

I froze. Canceled reservations because of the murders? That could mean financial disaster for Rose.

"I assumed that next week's invasion by Paul's television crew would never happen, and then I've overheard snatches of the phone calls you've been receiving."

"Somehow, the news of Paul's murder got out to the media already," Rose said. "But I'm sure the cancellations from the squeamish visitors will be offset by Paul's fans who will want to come and see where he met his end." Her voice was bitter as she added, "The ghouls."

"What will you do?"

"Ride it out. The murderer will be caught, and the inn will get back to normal."

"What about Emma? What if she decides to leave?"

The sound of fingernails tapping the arm of a chair drifted up to my balcony. If the conversation was turning to me, I didn't want to hear any more. I stood as quietly as I could and headed for my door, but Tim complained with a meow. I don't know how Rose answered Clara, because I scooted inside as quickly as I could and eased the door closed. Hopefully, they didn't realize I had been listening.

Carrying Tim in my arms, I paced around my small living room. This whole thing was getting out of hand. One murder was bad enough, but when you added Mary's poisoning and Paul's murder, it seemed like we were in the middle of a television murder mystery.

Tim squirmed in my arms, then batted at my face to let me know he was tired of being carried. His paw hit my nose giving me a reminder of my bruised face. I set Tim on the sectional then went to check my sore nose in the bathroom mirror. The redness had faded over the past couple days, and I had been able to mask most of it with makeup.

Everything looked fine. Tim's paw must have hit a sore spot. The way that door had hit me the other morning, I was surprised my nose wasn't broken.

The break-in. With everything that had happened with Mary and Paul, I had almost forgotten it had happened. That morning, Wil had been furious that his laptop had been stolen, but he hadn't said anything about it since then. Hadn't he told Cal that it had been stolen?

I checked my watch. It was a little after ten o'clock, so Wil was probably in his apartment. I went down the hall to the door marked "private" and rapped on it.

Wil pulled the door open. "What do you want?"

Then he grinned that crooked grin.

"I was just thinking about the intruder we had the other morning. Did you ever find your laptop?"

"Laptop?"

"Yeah. You said it had been stolen from the kitchen."

"No, I didn't say it had been stolen." He scrubbed a hand across the back of his neck. "It was in my apartment. I wouldn't leave it in the kitchen overnight."

I frowned. "But you were quite upset when you saw the drawer was open and the computer was gone. I remember."

He laughed. "You have quite an imagination, don't you? You and Rose are certainly related. She 'remembers' things that never happened, too." He gave me a crooked grin. "Come in and see. My laptop is on the kitchen island." Wil took a step back and opened the door wider. "You've never seen my place, have you?"

I took a few steps into the apartment. It had an open floor plan with the main room containing a sitting area, dining table, and a well-appointed kitchen. The computer was on the island countertop, just as he had said.

A door to the right led into a bedroom, and the door on the left, in the corner of the kitchen, had to be the one that led from the garage. Minimalist was the word for Wil's living room. It could have been taken from a magazine.

"Nice place," I said. "I like the dormer window. It gives you the perfect spot for reading." Wil had placed a Scandinavian design recliner in the alcove with a modern floor lamp hanging over it. "It looks very chic. Is that a genuine Ekornes chair?"

"I wouldn't have one of those cheap copies." Wil waved one hand toward the sofa in the center of the room. Its gray upholstery and modern lines complemented the Ekornes. "Have a seat. Can I get you something? A glass of wine?"

"No thanks. I can't stay long. I'm meeting Becky for lunch."

I bit my tongue at the lie I told, but I did plan to touch base with Becky before lunch. I perched on the couch as Wil joined me.

"So, your laptop wasn't stolen after all? You must be relieved that you didn't lose your recipes."

"Um. Yeah. Well, I have them backed up on the Cloud, but I still didn't want them to fall into a competitor's hands."

"They're just recipes, aren't they? I mean, you can get recipes from any cookbook, can't you?" I smiled as I spoke, knowing I was baiting the poor guy, but I couldn't resist the jab.

"Yeah. Whatever." His gaze shifted toward the kitchen as he eased forward on his seat.

He looked at me, then studied his hands. "Say, Emma, I was wondering if you were busy tomorrow night. Nothing is going on here at the inn, so I thought we could go get a bite to eat. Get to know each other a little better."

A fist closed in my chest as I fought to keep my breathing even. I tried to smile again.

"I don't date coworkers."

Not since Bruce.

"Don't call it a date. Call it a night out with a friend."

He smiled back at me, but was it just my imagination or did his smile end at his cheekbones? His eyes reminded me of Bruce's. Deep. Dark. Obsidian. A snake's eyes.

I blinked. Wil's eyes were just fine. Green with a touch of gray. Almost hazel.

"Sorry. I have plans." I mentally thanked Cal for giving me a good excuse, but why was I so reluctant to spend time with Wil?

"Maybe another time, then."

His voice was smooth. There was no threatening tone in his words. But the fist in my chest clenched tighter.

"Look, Wil." I took a deep breath. "I had a bad experience with a coworker once, and I don't want to risk repeating that mistake." I tried to give him a friendly smile. "I'd rather not go out with you. I hope you understand."

"Sure." He shrugged his shoulders as he stood. "Whatever you want."

I took his cue and headed for the door. "Thanks for inviting me in. You do have a lovely apartment."

"I like it." He opened the door for me. "I'm going out tonight, so I'll see you in the morning."

"Yup. I'll see you then." I slipped past him and into the hall. "Someday you'll have to give me the secret of how you make that wonderful coffee."

He grinned as he closed the door. I leaned against the wall, trying to breathe normally. What a strange encounter. The fist in my chest unclenched a little. Was my reaction only because of my memories of Bruce, or was there some undercurrent with Wil that affected me like this?

Eleven

My phone vibrated in my back pocket, making me jump. It was Cal. I answered it as I walked across the lounge to my suite.

"Hi Cal. Thanks for returning my call." I closed the door and leaned against it.

"What do you need?"

"I found a packet of arsenic in the greenhouse." Tim jumped down from the sectional and wound himself around my legs.

"A packet?"

"An envelope, really. About the size of an index card. And the label had been typed on the same typewriter as the notes."

Tim meowed and stalked into the kitchenette to his empty dish. I scooped some kibble into his bowl and freshened his water while I waited for Cal's answer.

"Where did you find this, exactly?"

"In the cabinet where Rose keeps her gardening tools."

"You didn't open it?"

"No, of course not." While Tim crunched his food, I plopped down on my sectional. "Don't you think it's suspicious that I found it with Rose's things?"

"Suspicious? Why?"

"Well, Rose uses arsenic in her garden, and the label was written with the typewriter. Could she -" I lowered my voice to a whisper. "-be the murderer?"

"Look, Emma." He paused and I heard a deep sigh. I could imagine him shoving his fingers through his hair. "This murderer has been planting evidence all over the place to lead the investigation where he wants it to go. We have no reason to suspect that Rose is the culprit any more than you are."

"But-"

"I'll stop by the inn this afternoon or in the morning to check it out. Meanwhile, don't tell anyone about what you found."

"Oh." I fidgeted with the hem of my t-shirt. "I already told Becky."

"Then tell her to keep it quiet."

"Sure." I hoped I wasn't too late. It seemed that no one kept secrets in Paragon.

"I'll catch up with you later."

"Okay."

"And stay safe."

"I'll try."

We ended the call. I stared at the phone in my hand. Stay safe? How was I supposed to do that with a murderer on the loose?

But meanwhile, we had an inn to run. Since Paul's death there would be no show filmed at the mine and no television crew to fill the inn. Even so, I needed to check our inventory and get ready for the next week. Perhaps we would have some last-minute guests.

I checked the time. I had an hour before heading to the café to talk to Becky, so I went down to the storeroom.

As I was in the middle of counting rolls of toilet paper, Rose came into the room. I couldn't meet her eyes, despite Cal's reassurances, but she didn't seem to notice.

"Emma, dear, I'm glad you're here." She was smiling and I put all thoughts of the envelope in the greenhouse out of my mind. "I wanted to talk to you about something."

"Sure." I looked around the room full of supplies. "Right now?"

She laughed, sounding happy and normal, as if three people hadn't been killed in the past week.

"Don't look so worried. Let's go out to the dining room. I'm ready for a cup of tea."

I grabbed a bottle of water from the small fridge on the buffet while Rose made her tea, then we sat at one of the round tables.

"How do you like your job here so far?" Rose stirred some sweetener into her cup.

"It's only been a week." I unscrewed the top of my bottle and took a sip.

"And it's been quite a week, hasn't it?" Rose's face sobered. "I'm so sorry. I'm sure you're beginning to think the inn is a disaster. You deserved to have a better beginning with us."

"I don't think any of us expected to have three deaths."

Rose turned her cup in her hand, a lovely mug decorated with blue columbines. "You're not thinking of leaving, are you?"

"Of course not." I smiled to erase the concern on my aunt's face. "I'm glad you asked me to work here this summer, and I wouldn't think of leaving before fall."

"That brings me to what I wanted to talk to you about."

I braced myself. That sounded like the preamble to my walking papers.

"I've made an appointment with my solicitor for tomorrow morning."

"Solicitor? You mean your lawyer?"

"I'm going to change my will." She looked at me. "I want to name you as my heir."

I leaned back in my chair, and my astonishment must have shown on my face because Rose smiled.

"I know I should have discussed this with you earlier, but with things the way they are, I wanted to get this taken care of as soon as possible."

"You mean because it looks like someone is targeting you."

"Yes." She sipped her tea. "Despite what Montgomery says, I have my share of enemies that even he doesn't know about. I no longer think the events of this week are necessarily connected with my past, but they have reminded me that life is just as uncertain now as it was before I retired. The book I'm writing has many people very worried."

"You really think your life is in jeopardy because of your memoirs?"

Rose nodded. "I decided early on that I would expose secrets that have been hidden too long. That's a dangerous thing in my business."

I scooted closer and leaned on the table. "Rose, I need to know. Have you ever, well, killed anyone?"

"Does it make a difference to you if I did?"

Her face lost all color, and her strong and capable hands suddenly looked as fragile as the porcelain cup they were clasping.

"No." I realized as I said it that it was the truth. "I would love you no matter what. I've always known that you supported me, even when Dad kept me from writing to you or calling for all those years."

"Thank you, Emma." She grasped my hand. "I needed to hear that, especially from you." She released my hand and stirred her tea. "And the answer is yes. I have killed when it was necessary."

"Necessary?" Doubt knocked. When was it ever necessary to kill someone?

"When I needed to protect someone, yes, it was necessary."

"But now you think your life is in danger."

"I know it is. Montgomery gives me some protection while he's here, but he won't be with me all the time."

"And Clara?"

Rose smiled and drank some tea. "Dear Clara. She would lay her life down to save mine."

I believed her.

"Emma, will you be my heir? It means that when I die-"

"If you die, you mean."

"No dear. Sooner or later, death comes to all of us. When I die, you would own my part of the inn and all my assets, except for the parts of my estate that will be donated to charity." She turned her gaze on me, once again sharp and clear. "The most important task you will have, though, is to publish my memoirs. I already have an agreement with a publisher, but you will need to see that everything is done the right way."

I began to see what she was asking of me.

"If you think I can handle the responsibility, I will do it."

"I have no doubt about your capabilities." She finished her tea. "Now, we should celebrate, don't you think? Why don't you come into town with me in the morning after the guests leave? The appointment with my solicitor is at eleven o'clock. After I sign the papers, we'll have lunch in town."

"That sounds great. I'm looking forward to it."

As Rose went back to her suite, I checked my watch. I had enough time to finish the toilet paper inventory before heading down to the café to talk to Becky. I found my clipboard and started counting, but a noise from the kitchen interrupted me. Thinking it was just Wil, I found my place again and kept counting.

I was writing down the number when I heard the noise again. This time it was more distinct, like someone slamming a pan down on a counter. It sounded like Wil was having a bad day. I crossed the hall and pushed the kitchen door open an inch. Wil was standing with his back to me, leaning on the prep counter, his shoulders heaving. Was he crying? I almost stepped into the room, but then he slammed his fist on the prep counter. I backed away and let the door swing shut. I wasn't about to confront creepy Wil in the middle of his temper tantrum.

Checking my watch again, I put the clipboard on its peg and headed toward the café. I had a half-hour before the noon lunch rush, so Becky should be available.

When I arrived, Becky was sitting in one of the chairs that lined the front porch.

"I thought you'd be busy prepping for the lunch rush," I said as I sat in the chair next to her.

"Everything is ready, and I found some help. You wouldn't believe how many of Angie's friends thought it would be fun to work a shift at the café." She leaned back in her chair. "I decided it was time for me to take a break." She nudged my foot with hers. "Did you get in touch with Cal? What did he say about the arsenic you found?"

"He agreed with you, that it was probably planted in Rose's cupboard by the real murderer."

Becky grinned. "I told you. So, why did you come by? Did you want to work the lunch shift, too?"

"It sounds like you have that covered." I paused. How did you tell someone that the guy she likes creeps you out? I cleared my throat. "It's about Wil."

"He isn't hurt or anything, is he?" Her eyes widened. "Or did you two have a fight? You're worse than siblings, you know that don't you?"

"No, it isn't anything like that." I bit my lip, then shook my head. I had to just tell her. "He asked me to have supper with him tomorrow night."

"What?" Becky stood up. "I've been waiting for months for him to ask me out. I had almost decided he's immune to my charms. How did you get him to do it?" She frowned at me. "You didn't say you would, did you?"

I shook my head. "That's what I wanted to tell you. I told him I don't date coworkers, but I wouldn't go out with him anyway."

"Why not? He's the catch of the century."

"Sit down." I patted her chair. "It's a long story, but it has to do with a guy named Bruce that I used to date in St. Kitts. It became a nightmare. I almost didn't get away from him alive."

"I had no idea."

"I don't tell many people about it."

"How long were you together?"

"Almost two years. At the end, I felt like I was losing my mind."

"What happened to him?"

"He was arrested, then I was transferred to Cancun. I haven't seen him since." I took a deep breath. "But the point is that Wil reminded me of Bruce this morning." I shivered.

"How?"

"Something about the look in his eyes."

"Are you sure it isn't just your imagination? Maybe Wil was coming on a little strong, so your brain connected him with the bad experience you had with Bruce."

"I don't think so. Part of it was the way he asked me out. Out of the blue, like he had just thought of it. Most guys don't ask girls out on the spur of the moment. It takes them time to work up to it."

Becky shrugged. "I wouldn't know."

"Hey." I nudged her shoulder. "I didn't tell you this to depress you. I thought you needed to know what I saw. If someone had warned me about Bruce, I could have avoided what he put me through."

"You don't know that Wil is the same as this Bruce guy." Becky got up and started toward the café door. "Remember, you don't know Wil like I do."

The screen door slapped behind her as she went into the restaurant. That slap felt like a dash of cold water. Becky was right. I didn't know Wil very well, and I didn't know her well yet, either. She reacted the same way I would have if someone had told me how dangerous Bruce was. I hadn't seen it until it was too late.

Had I lost Becky as a friend? I started walking back to the inn. I hoped I hadn't, and I wasn't going to give up on her. What kind of friend would I be if I was right about Wil's creepiness, but didn't say anything to warn Becky? I sighed. Not much of one, that was for sure.

Meanwhile, the murderer was still somewhere. Was he or she planning another death?

I turned up the inn's driveway. The past few days had been full of activity, but where were the clues? The culprit was leading me around like a dog on a leash, only letting me see what he wanted me to see.

That had to stop. Now.

Once I got to my suite, I made myself a tuna salad sandwich and grabbed an apple. I sat on the sectional and opened my bullet journal on the ottoman. As I ate, I read through the lists I had made through the week.

As I scanned the list of guests, I added in details I had learned since I had first written it. Annie's experience with Paul. Roger's reaction to the news. Sam...

I tapped the pen against my chin. It seemed that every detail about Sam and Nora tended to contradict the next one. At first, they were interested in exploring old mines. Then they became enamored with the casinos and shopping and seemed to forget pursuing lost gold. But the expenses they must have incurred to hire Dead Dick told me they wouldn't have given up that quest easily. What was the real motive for their trip here? And then they had been quiet when they returned to the inn the last two days. What did they do during the day? Innocent sightseeing? Or was there something about the Graves' Folly mine that they were involved in?

The mine. I turned to a fresh page in my journal. All week I had had the feeling that this mystery revolved around the mine. I listed the details about Graves' Folly that Becky had told me.

When I wrote, *no gold found,* I underlined it twice. Why would an old mine that had never yielded any gold a hundred years ago be responsible for three deaths today? I started a list of possibilities on the right-hand side of the page. Maybe someone had discovered the rich vein that Becky's great-grandfather had never found. Perhaps there was another mineral that the original owners hadn't been aware of. But what, other than gold, would be valuable enough to kill someone over?

Buried treasure? I almost crossed that one out but left it. There wouldn't be a pirate's treasure, but could there be gold from a stagecoach robbery back in the days of the Old West? Hadn't Sam and Nora mentioned something like that?

I leafed through the pages again and sighed. As far as I could tell, everything was random. Nothing to connect the details. I took my dishes back to the kitchenette and grabbed the clue board that Becky and I had set up and laid it on the ottoman. Still nothing. I tried standing up and looking at it from different angles until my brain felt like mush. I needed Becky to help. The ideas always came faster when she was around.

It was after the lunch rush. I texted her to see if she could come over. My thumb hovered over the send button, remembering Becky's hurt feelings when we talked before lunch. Was she over them yet? I tapped the screen and sent the message. The worst that could happen was that she didn't return my message.

When her answer, give me fifteen minutes, came back almost immediately, I grinned to myself. Our friendship had survived the first disagreement.

While I waited, I went on with my work. The inventory could wait, but the sweeping had to get done before the guests arrived back at the inn this afternoon. I started in the upstairs lounge, using the small vacuum on the area rugs before dust mopping the hardwood floors. As I ran the sweeper over the large center rug, it picked up something embedded in the carpet that clicked and rattled in the machine.

I turned off the vacuum and knelt to examine the rug. Had someone walked through the room with dirty shoes? Some gravel was embedded in the carpet's deep pile. I picked a few out. The stones were sharp rather than rounded. Where had I seen something like this before? I held one up. Was it quartz? Or granite? Shiny flecks were ingrained in the stone. I picked up a few more. They were tiny, less than a quarter inch across, but they were all the same.

Were they another clue? I took the stones I had picked up into my suite and laid them on the counter, then went back to my vacuuming. The rattling continued all the way across the rug toward Sam and Nora's room, and the trail of tiny stones continued across the hardwood floor and under their door. I took my phone out of my pocket and snapped a photo. It could be nothing, but at least I'd have a record of what I found.

When I went downstairs to get the broom and dustpan, I met Becky coming in the front door.

"Hey, girl," she said. "What's up?"

"I need your help in a brainstorming session, but first I need to sweep up a mess."

We went back upstairs where she held the dustpan for me while I swept up the stones from the hardwood floor.

"These would destroy the floor if someone walked on them," Becky said, stirring the sharp pieces in the dustpan with her finger.

"The trail leads across the carpet to Sam and Nora's room."

"But you didn't find any on the stairs?"

I looked behind us. "That's right. They didn't show up until I started vacuuming the rug." I took the dustpan from Becky. "Let's go into my suite."

While she greeted Tim, I found a small dish and poured the stones from the dustpan into it. Becky came over and picked one up, examining it like I had earlier.

"Do they look familiar to you? I know I've seen stones like this before."

"Sure. This is quartz with mica mixed in. You'll find it everywhere in this part of the Black Hills."

"Everywhere?"

She held one of the larger stones between her thumb and forefinger. "These are what we used to call 'calicoes' when I was a kid. See the brown, red, and gold mixed in?"

"Sam and Nora must have carried a bunch of rocks into their room and dropped these on the way." I went into my living room and wrote the information under Sam's and Nora's names. "And now we have another piece to the puzzle that doesn't fit."

Becky sat next to me, examining our board. "Almost everyone has something written under their name."

"That's right. Each of us has a clue that's connected to us. But there's more."

I added my name to the board and wrote that the typewriter had been found in my closet. Then I wrote down Rose's name and the information about the packet of arsenic I had found.

"Should we add your name?" I glanced at Becky. "Are there any clues that point to you?"

She shook her head. "Not one. The clues all seem to be centered around people who are staying or work at the inn."

"Except for Montgomery and Clara."

We both stared at the board in silence.

Becky sighed. "Nothing makes sense. Nothing is connected."

"You're right. We have Annie's confession that Paul was the father of her child, which gives both her and Roger motives for killing Paul, but nothing to connect them to Mary and Dick."

"And then the stones we found today seem to point to Sam and Nora, but only to connect them to the mine."

I began to see a pattern. "We know the typewriter was planted in my room. What if all these clues were planted?"

"Why would someone do that?"

"To throw us off the trail. To confuse things."

Becky waved her hand across the board. "Do you mean all of these clues are fake?"

"No. Some of them, or all of them, might be real, but planted to point us in the direction the murderer wants us to go."

"So, we're back to square one." She slumped against the back of the couch.

"Not quite. We still have all the clues. We just need to see where they lead us." I opened my bullet journal to a new page and wrote "Clues" across the top. "First is the typewriter found in my closet."

"Wait." Becky sat up again. "Put them in the order that you found them. The murderer is trying to throw us off by jumbling them up and using them to point to certain people."

"You're right."

I started listing the clues in the order we found them, leaving blank lines to add in anything we might have forgotten to put on the clue board. When I finished, I tapped the notebook with the end of my pen, thinking.

Becky twisted her ponytail in one hand. "It still doesn't make any sense to me."

"One thing does, though." I pointed at a few items on the list. "Look how many things are connected to the mine. The rocks we found today, Paul's death, Dick's death."

"We don't know that Dick's death is connected to the mine."

I remembered the rose quartz and the lichen Cal had found under my sectional and added them to the list.

"It might be circumstantial, but it looks like Dick was somewhere near the mine. Remember, Sam and Nora had hired him to take them to a few mines in the area."

"There are items that could be connected to the notes Rose received, too." Becky pointed them out: the notes, the typewriter, the label on the arsenic packet.

I groaned. "Now it's becoming as confusing as ever."

My phone rang with the "Dragnet" theme I had downloaded and attached to Cal's number.

"Hey, Cal."

"There have been some developments in the case."

"What kind of developments?"

He ignored my question. "I need to talk to all the residents of the inn. I'll bring a couple officers and we'll question everyone tonight. Can you make sure they will all be there at five o'clock?"

"That's right in the middle of our afternoon tea. As far as I know, everyone is planning to attend. It's the last night for the Smiths and the Nelsons."

"We'll need to talk to the staff, too."

"Rose and I will be here, but I don't know about Wil. He said something about being busy tonight."

"I'll contact him directly and make sure he's there."

"Can you tell me what the new developments are?"

He hung up.

"What was that all about?" Becky's eyes were wide, looking as mystified as I felt.

"Cal is bringing some officers with him to the inn this afternoon to question all the guests and staff."

"What about?"

I shrugged. "He said there were some new developments in the case."

Becky glanced at our clue board. "Maybe he'll have more clues for us."

"Or he thinks he knows who the murderer is."

"Does he need me to be here, too?"

"He said he needed to talk to the guests and the staff, so I guess that leaves you out."

"I don't think I've ever been happier to be excluded from something."

I checked my watch. "I have an hour before I need to get the afternoon tea set up. Do you want to go for a walk with me?"

"Where?"

"Back up to the mine. The forensics team is finished with their work, and I'd like to refresh my memory of the mine and the overlook before I talk to Cal."

"Sure thing."

As we left the room, I looked back to make sure I hadn't left anything out that Tim would bother. The cat stared at me from his perch on the back of the couch and blinked both eyes as if to say, "I've got it under control." I grinned and closed the door. That cat never had anything under control.

Twelve

When we reached the overlook, I peeked over the edge. No body. No red scarf. I looked at the bottom of the cliff for several minutes, hoping the new view would help erase the image of Paul's broken body that still appeared in my memory.

"What did you think you'd find?" Becky asked, joining me at the cliff's edge. "Cal's forensics team combed this place thoroughly. I don't see anything you wouldn't expect to see here."

"I don't know. But both Dick and Paul were killed up here near the mine. I'm sure of it." I stepped back and looked at the mountains surrounding us. "What is it about this place that made someone kill three people?"

Becky shrugged. "It's the same as it's always been. We could be here at any time in the past hundred years, and we would see exactly the same things. Trees, mountains, rocks, granite spires, rimrock." She pointed to a bird soaring above us. "And bald eagles."

I watched the eagle. The quiet of the wilderness was broken only by the sound of the wind in the pines. My throat filled with an emotion I couldn't fathom. A nameless longing.

"It's beautiful," I said, my voice a whisper.

Becky grinned. "You've caught it."

"What?"

"The power of the wilderness. You'll never be happy in a city again."

As we walked back to the inn, I considered Becky's words. Rose's plan for me to stay at the Sweetbrier meant I wouldn't have to leave. Ever. I could make my home here. With that thought, that nameless longing I had felt on the overlook was fulfilled. I would have a home here in the Black Hills. I did a little dance in the middle of the road.

"What?" Becky asked, grabbing my hands and joining the dance.

"I'm just so happy to be here, even with everything that's happened."

We continued our dance down the hill. Laughing and exhausted, we said goodbye at the inn's driveway. Becky went on home as I went in to prepare for the afternoon tea.

Becky had brought frosted orange scones with the delivery that morning. I laid them out on the serving tray, then made a fresh pot of coffee. I checked the tea bag containers and replenished the packets of sweeteners and poured fresh pitchers of cream, milk, and half and half. A stack of plates, forks, and napkins, and we were all set. I knocked on Rose's door. Thatcher barked.

It took a few minutes for her to open the door. She was wearing reading glasses on a chain around her neck and her favorite violet cardigan.

"Emma? Is anything wrong?"

"Not at all. I just wanted to tell you that Cal will be here at five o'clock with some other deputies. He said he had some developments in the case and wants to talk to everyone."

Rose's glance flickered toward her office door, which was standing open. "What time is it now?" She rubbed her face as if she was trying to wake herself up.

"It's four-fifteen. Were you sleeping? I'm sorry if I disturbed you."

"Oh, no, dear." She thrust her glasses into the pocket of her sweater. "I was writing. I lose track of the time when I get lost in the narrative. Old memories, you know. I'll be out to join you for tea soon."

Thatcher jumped up on her leg and whined.

Rose rubbed his head. "Poor boy. I haven't taken him out since this morning."

"I have a few minutes. Let me do it."

Thatcher trotted ahead of me to the door, then out to the small space to the right of the walkway where he took care of his business.

While I waited, I looked up at Grizzly Peak across the road from the inn. The tall, straight trunks of the Ponderosa pines were interspersed with granite outcroppings on the steep mountainside that rose three hundred or more feet above the road. A trail I hadn't noticed before threaded up the side. As I watched, a figure appeared where the trail rounded the edge of the mountain and came down toward the road. It was Wil.

Thatcher finished what he was doing and scratched at the dirt with his hind legs. Then he spotted Wil. Barking, he ran out toward the driveway.

"Thatcher, stop that." The dog stopped at the end of the cement apron, but still watched Wil coming down the trail, gruffing at him.

"I didn't know you were a hiker," I called to Wil as he came closer.

"I was just out for a walk when the deputy called me."

"Then he got in touch with you."

"You know about this?"

"Sure. He's going to talk to all of us." I waved as the Nelsons' rental car drove into the parking lot, followed by the Smith's blue Kia. "And the guests have arrived home just in time. Are you going to join us for tea? It's the last one before they leave tomorrow.

He shot me a look that reminded me he didn't associate with the guests. "Are you kidding? I'll be down when the police arrive."

Wil let himself in the entry door by the garage while I took Thatcher into the inn. Rose, Clara, and Montgomery were all standing in the foyer. Rose took Thatcher into her suite.

I greeted Rose's friends. "Did Rose tell you that we're having visitors this afternoon?"

"Visitors?" Nora and Sam came in the door behind me. "Who?"

Annie and Roger were right behind them.

"Deputy Cal and some other officers want to talk to us about some new developments in the case. They'll be here in about thirty minutes."

I couldn't help noticing the glances that passed between Sam and Nora. Annie and Roger, too.

"But now it's time for tea." I kept my voice bright and engaging. "You can tell us about the sights you've seen today."

I ushered all of them into the dining room where they helped themselves to drinks. Only Sam and Nora took a scone for each of them. Rose joined us, but no one spoke. They sat in their chairs.

"Did you all enjoy your last day in the Black Hills?"

No one answered me. Sam and Nora finished their scones while Roger and Annie drank ice water.

"Sam, did you find any new casinos on your rambles today?"

He shook his head, then stared at me. "What is the deputy going to question us about, anyway? We didn't have anything to do with the murders that have been happening around here."

"They just want to talk to us. We might have seen or heard something that will help the investigation."

We waited. Rose and Clara talked about the crocuses blooming in the garden, and Rose invited everyone to see the greenhouse before they checked out in the morning.

Sam drummed his fingers on the wooden surface while Nora attacked her nails with an emery board. Montgomery sat next to Rose. Every so often he moved a hand toward her, as if he wanted to comfort her, then drew it back. Clara sat on the other side of Rose, stirring tea that must have been tepid by now.

I took a seat at the fourth table, and a few minutes before five, Wil took the chair across from me, staring at his phone. He didn't even glance at me.

Was the murderer one of the people in this room? I shifted in my chair. I had spent the past week with these people, guests of the inn. I didn't want to think any of them could be capable of murder.

Cal finally came in, followed by three other officers, two women and a man. He set his duffel bag on the only empty table and laid his hat next to it.

"I'll need a statement from each one of you-"

"You can't think one of us murdered Paul, can you?" Sam's angry burst interrupted Cal's steady voice.

I was impressed that the deputy remained calm. "I didn't say that any of you was a suspect, but all of you are witnesses." He turned to Rose. "Are there a couple rooms that will give us some privacy for the interviews? Deputy Thompson will be doing some while I handle the rest, and Officers Wilson and Smith will assist us. We will try to make the process as quick and painless as possible."

"You can use my suite," Rose said, then glanced at me.

"And mine," I said, trying to appear calm. "I'll put Tim in his carrier so he doesn't bother you."

The evening dragged on as each of the guests was interviewed and then released to go about their business. Wil, Rose, and I were the last ones.

Finally, Cal called me upstairs. When I entered my living room, Cal was sitting on one L of my sectional while Officer Smith stood behind it, in the same spot where we had found Dick's body.

"Do you think the three murders are connected?" I asked as I sat on the other leg of the couch. "You have to admit, two dead bodies and a death from poison can't be a coincidence."

Cal cleared his throat. "Do I have to remind you that this is an interview? It's customary for me to ask the questions and for you to answer them."

"Come on, Cal, you don't think I'm a suspect again, do you?"

"I can't overlook the fact that you found both bodies, and you found the poisoned food." Cal shuffled through some plastic bags and placed one on the ottoman in front of me. "Do you recognize this?"

"It looks like the paper we found under Mary's bed."

I read the two messages that were written on it out loud. The first one, in masculine handwriting said, "I know an expensive secret. You'll want to talk to me about it." Typed below that was, "10:30. The overlook."

"It looks like Paul was blackmailing the murderer," Cal said. "Not a very smart thing to do."

"Why are we going over this again?"

"We found the murder weapon in Paul's death. He was bludgeoned with a piece of wood, then either fell or was pushed off the overlook."

As Cal watched me, I wondered what my face was revealing. Probably just my sick stomach. After a minute, Cal pulled another evidence bag from his duffel and tossed it onto the ottoman.

"A rock?"

"That was clutched in his hand."

"Why? I mean, he was falling, right?" The image of Paul falling backward off the cliff was haunting. "It seems like a person in those, um, circumstances would be trying to reach out to grab something, don't you think? Could he have caught himself, even for a second on the edge of the cliff, and that rock broke off?"

"I thought of that." Cal pulled another bag from his duffel. "But this is a sample from the rimrock at the edge of the cliff. If you compare the two, you can see how different they are."

He was right. The piece from the rimrock was sandy colored, even reddish, and was solid. The piece from Paul's hand sparkled and was slightly crumbly.

"This looks familiar." I pointed to the red, brown, and yellow flecks mingled with shiny bits in the stone. "Becky called this calico quartz."

"It's quartz with mica in it. The questions I have are where did Paul get that rock and why was it so important that he held onto it?"

"I have one more question," I said as I handed the evidence bags back to him. "What is the connection with Dick's murder?"

"Dick was a geologist."

"And Paul was holding a rock. But that isn't much of a connection."

"Maybe they both found the same rock," Officer Smith said.

Cal and I both stared at her. She had been so quiet that I had forgotten she was in the room.

"The same rock?" Cal asked.

"Or the same kind of rock." The officer answered.

I went into the kitchen and grabbed the container of stones I had found in the carpet that morning.

"These were on the floor when I was vacuuming this morning. There was a trail that led across the carpet in the second-floor lobby to Sam and Nora's room. It was obviously planted since there weren't any on the stairs or anywhere else." I opened the file on my phone and showed Cal the picture.

"Is there something special about it?" Officer Smith asked.

Cal shrugged. "It's just quartz. You can find it all over the Black Hills."

"No," I said. "It isn't just quartz. It's quartz worth killing for. We have to find out why."

Cal and the others finished up their work and left. I was so tired that I didn't go back downstairs. I let Tim out of his crate and sat on the sectional.

One thing I was discovering was that solving a mystery was nothing like my favorite television shows. In those stories, there was always a clear path from the crime to the perpetrator. The sleuth only had to sort out the real clues from the red herrings and the case was done. All in less than an hour. Even in mystery stories I could pick up the trail of clues the author had left and solve the crime by the end.

But nothing was clear about Dick's murder, and Paul's just added a new layer of mud to the mess. And why was Mary killed?

I opened my bullet journal. Maybe the answer could be found in the connections between the suspects.

I started with Dick. He had been hired by Sam and Nora to tour old mines in the area. Rose- Wait, was Rose a suspect? I frowned. Cal said everyone was a suspect, so yes, I needed to include Rose's connection to him through his community education classes, and Becky's and Gran's connection to him through the café.

No one else had known him, as far as I knew.

Paul was a different story. Everyone knew Paul, or at least knew of him, because of his television show. Annie had an intimate connection with him, though. She had sounded very hurt and angry when I overheard her talking to him about the child he had fathered. And what about Roger? Would he feel betrayed enough to commit murder?

Then there was that note I found under Mary's bed. It looked like Paul was blackmailing someone, but who? And why?

I drew careful square boxes in the margin of the page as I considered the question.

What connected the victims? Dick was dead before Paul and Mary even arrived at the inn last Friday, so they probably hadn't met.

Or were we looking at two different murderers?

I leaned back and closed my eyes. Too many details. Tim uttered a questioning meow just before he jumped onto my lap, so I moved my journal over and stroked his sleek fur as he settled in. Fuzz therapy was the best. I put my feet up on the couch and reclined against the arm. Tim purred as I relaxed, letting my mind clear.

The image of the piece of quartz Cal had found clutched in Paul's hand remained. Where had I seen a rock like that before today?

My eyes popped open. The mine. Becky's fairy sparkles. Could that be where Paul found his sparkling piece of calico quartz?

I got up with the sun on Saturday morning, which meant I was late. Way late. And on the final morning for this group of guests. Great. Just when we needed to leave them with a stellar final experience. Reviews were everything in this business.

By the time I reached the kitchen, Becky and Wil were already sparring.

"Where's the coffee?" I asked as I ran my fingers through my damp hair. No time for the blow dryer this morning.

"There isn't any," Becky said, handing me her invoice to sign. "Mister Super-Chef is in a bad mood."

I glanced at Wil. He stood at the other end of the counter spooning a cheesy spinach filling onto squares of puff pastry.

"I'm not in a bad mood." His voice came out as a growl.

"That noise this morning must have kept him awake. Poor baby didn't get enough sleep."

"What noise?" I asked.

"You didn't hear it?" Becky leaned on the end of the worktable. "It was like a sonic boom, or an explosion. Around three o'clock this morning."

"I heard something, but I thought it was thunder and went back to sleep."

Wil gave us one of his long-suffering sighs. "Yeah. I heard it. I thought it sounded like a gunshot from a high-powered rifle. Probably poachers. I'll give Game, Fish, and Parks a call." He turned his back to us. "Now leave me alone. I'm busy."

"Too busy to chat with a friend?" Becky raised her chin in a gesture that said she was ready for an argument.

Wil stopped his work and gave her a look that told me I needed to get Becky out of there before they came to blows.

"Come on, Becky. Let's get some coffee in the dining room." I took the invoice with me and grabbed a pen from the reception desk.

"What's going on with the two of you?" I asked as I started the coffee maker.

Becky plopped herself onto a chair. "I have no idea. He was in a bad mood when I came in."

I signed the invoice and looked it over before I handed it to her. "It seems funny to have no scones on the list."

"It seemed funny not to make them. But Rose called and said there was no need, with only four of you here this afternoon."

"She's right. The Nelsons and the Smiths are checking out this morning, and we don't have any other guests checking in."

The first pot of coffee finished brewing and I started a second before I poured myself a cup. I looked at Becky and held the pot up.

"No thanks. I've got to get back to the café. Angie is still sick today, so I'm filling in for her again. Want to give me a hand?"

"I can't." I took a sip of the coffee. It was good, but not anywhere close to Wil's masterpiece. "Rose and I have an appointment in town, then we're going out for lunch."

A loud bang sounded from behind the closed shutter.

Becky stood up, folding the invoice. "It sounds like Wil's mood hasn't improved. I hope this doesn't mean he's decided to poison breakfast."

"Don't even joke about something like that." I shuddered.

"Oh, right. Sorry." She patted my shoulder. "By the way, did Cal arrest anyone last night?"

I shook my head. "He only talked to everyone."

"Questioned them, you mean."

"Okay. Questioned. But when he talked to me, he didn't mention much about the murders. He seemed curious about a rock they had found in Paul's hand, though."

"What kind of rock?"

"The same as those stones we found upstairs yesterday, but larger. In fact, I thought it looked like your fairy stones in the mine."

Becky grinned. "You know that's just a vein of quartz, right?"

"Calico quartz with mica mixed in, which is what makes it sparkle. There isn't anything special about that rock that you know of, is there?"

She shook her head. "It's so common, I don't even think about it when I see it. What did Cal say?"

"Nothing. I think he's stumped."

"That means he's still looking for the bad guy."

"He had better hurry and solve this case. If he suspects one of our guests, he's going to have to do something soon."

Soon after Becky left, Montgomery came down the stairs, as impeccably dressed as always.

"Good morning, Emma." He winked at me as he adjusted his cuff links. "Should I bring in the newspaper?"

"Oh, I forgot all about it."

"No worries," he said, heading toward the door. "I enjoy making myself useful."

I raised the shutter over the buffet counter. Wil was just taking a pan of the spinach and cheese puffs out of the oven.

"Should I set up the chafing rack for those?"

He glared at me. "What do you think?"

Man, he was in a bad mood. "If I knew, I wouldn't be asking you."

He gave a dramatic sigh. "No chafing rack. These are served at room temperature."

"Okay. Thanks." I paused. He was being a real pain this morning. Something had to take him out of this mood before the guests came downstairs. I pointed to the fruit he had just taken out of the cooler. "That fruit plate looks fabulous. Are you making a dressing for it?"

"Of course." His voice wasn't quite as sharp as he launched into his favorite subject: his food. "I tossed the fruit pieces in an orange, lemon, and honey dressing before I arranged them. This extra dressing will give the plate a fine glaze for serving."

Whatever he might have added to his soliloquy on the dressing was interrupted as Roger and Annie came downstairs.

"Good morning," I said. "The coffee and tea are ready. Have a seat. Breakfast will be up in just a few minutes."

Montgomery joined the couple as I went into the kitchen to transfer the cheese and spinach puffs to a serving platter. Sam and Nora appeared, arguing as they came into the dining room.

"We're heading home today, and that's the end of it," Nora said, leading the way to the coffee pot.

"But I'm going to ask Rose if we can stay here an extra week. If we can't, we'll find another place nearby."

"I've had it with the Black Hills, and I want to get home to Foofie. You know he just pines when we're away. I'm sure he hasn't eaten a thing all week." Nora turned on her husband, her face red, but faltered when she saw that we were all watching her. She touched her hairdo and smiled. "Foofie is our pug. He's delicate and needs special care."

Sam snorted. "You'll kill that dog with your special care. You know the vet said to lighten up. He's just fine at the kennel. I still have some business to take care of here."

Nora kept the smile pasted on her face as she nudged Sam. He turned and saw the rest of us.

"Good morning, folks. Don't mind us. Marital bliss, you know." He poured himself a cup of coffee and added plenty of sugar and cream.

"You two aren't leaving today?" Roger asked as Sam and Nora joined them at their table.

"Yes, we are," said Nora.

"No, we're not," said Sam at the same time.

"I guess it's still under discussion," said Annie. "We need to get home, though. Spring break is over, and school starts again on Monday."

"That's right." Nora stirred three packets of the blue sweetener into her coffee. "The two of you are teachers."

Annie nodded.

The front door opened, and Deputy Cal came in. My hopes for a stellar final morning dropped to the floor.

"Breakfast is ready," I said to the group as I made my way through the room to Cal. "Help yourselves."

"Are they all here?" Cal asked as he set his hat on the reception desk.

"Except for Clara and Rose. I saw them take Thatcher out a few minutes ago, so they will be back soon." I pointed to the fluorescent yellow box he was carrying. "What's that?"

His face was grim. No twinkle in his eye. Not even the ubiquitous toothpick. "A Geiger counter."

The implications made my stomach turn. "Was that rock radioactive?"

"Yup." He looked past me toward the guests chatting in the dining room. "Which ones are leaving today?"

"Annie and Roger definitely are. It seems that Sam and Nora are still discussing it. He wants to stay an extra week, but she wants to go home."

Cal walked past me and stood next to the coffee and tea station until he had everyone's attention.

"I need to ask you all for one more favor." He held up the Geiger counter. "I need to use this to test your clothes and your luggage. It won't take long."

"Isn't this a bit obtrusive, Officer?" Sam said. "I mean, what could we have that is radioactive?"

Rose and Clara came in the front door and joined me at the reception desk.

"Uranium." Cal shifted his grip on the Geiger counter.

Rose handed Thatcher's leash to Clara. "Uranium?" She moved into the dining room and stood behind Montgomery's chair. "Where did you find uranium?"

"I'll be testing your things, too." Cal didn't answer her question.

Rose nodded. "Whatever you need to do to get to the bottom of these murders."

The guests all nodded agreement, although Sam was hesitant until he saw he was the odd man out. They continued with their breakfasts as Cal went through Rose's suite, then Clara's.

I followed him with my keys in my hand as he went up the stairs.

At the top of the stairs, Cal switched the machine on. It emitted a steady stream of quiet clicks. The counter remained quiet until we reached the Albertine, the room Mary and Paul had shared. Then it reacted with loud static when he ran the sensor over Paul's briefcase.

"I expected that," Cal said. "Paul had the uranium rich rock in his possession."

Outside the Dublin Bay, Sam and Nora's room, the counter went crazy again.

"That's where I swept up the stones yesterday," I said. "There must still be some in the carpet."

When I opened the door, Cal took the counter in, and the clicking returned to normal.

"You were right. Those stones were another plant to distract us." Cal continued scanning their room with his machine. "It was a sloppy job, though. The murderer is getting careless."

"But that doesn't mean Sam and Nora can't be guilty, does it? They could have planted those stones that way on purpose, to make us think it wasn't them."

"Or that's your imagination talking."

Cal pushed past me and continued to my suite. The Agatha Christie rose on the door failed to calm my nerves as I turned the lever. Had the murderer left a surprise in here for us again?

The counter clicked and popped like crazy in the kitchenette as Cal went near the bowl of stones I had found yesterday, but the rest of my suite was clean.

"The only room left is Wil's apartment," I said.

I led the way past the Westerland to Wil's door. Cal rapped. No answer.

"Maybe he's still in the kitchen. I don't have a key to his place."

We went back downstairs. Wil had disappeared as he often did after breakfast had been served, but the guests were still in the dining room.

"Any luck?" Sam was in a better mood than he had been before. "Which one of us is the perp?"

"Inconclusive." Cal's answer seemed to satisfy him. Turning to me, he said, "If you see Wil, have him call me."

After the deputy left, Rose came up to me. "We need to leave soon to get to our appointment in time. Clara will look after things here."

"Have Sam and Nora decided if they're staying an extra week?"

"They are, so Roger and Annie are the only ones who are leaving today." She smiled. "Two guests are better than an empty inn, aren't they? But the Nelsons are planning to be gone all day, so no afternoon tea to prepare."

It only took a few minutes for me to freshen up and to say goodbye to Roger and Annie. They were both in a happy mood and promised to stay at the Sweetbrier again on their next trip to the Black Hills.

As I joined Rose in her Range Rover, she laughed. "I've never seen you smile so much."

"When a guest leaves happy, it's the best feeling, isn't it?"

"I can tell you are cut out for this business. Putting the guests' needs first is all important."

Rose backed out of the garage and headed down the drive. She turned left at the end of Graves' Gulch Road and headed toward Rapid City.

"I think you're right," I said. "I do enjoy meeting new people and making them comfortable. It's an aspect that I lost with all the pressure of my job with Votrejour International."

"Does this mean you're definitely staying?" Rose glanced at me then back at the road. "I must admit, I do have my hopes set on a long-term partnership. The three of us can make the Sweetbrier Inn into a Black Hills destination." Rose made another left turn onto a gravel road I didn't recognize. She glanced at me with a smile. "My favorite scenic short cut."

"Have you talked to Wil about bringing me on?"

"Yes."

Her short answer seemed filled with doubt.

"He isn't excited about the change, though?"

"Not yet." Rose shot a bright smile my way. "But he'll come around. He will see how my vision for the inn will help his career."

"He hasn't said anything about moving on?"

"No, and I hope-"

A sudden pop came just as Rose gasped and lost control of the car. The Range Rover skidded from one side of the road to the other, then headed off the gravel road and jolted down the slope toward a single large tree. The airbags deployed as we hit and came to an abrupt halt.

Dazed, I looked at Rose. Her eyes were closed. Blood covered her face and dripped down her arm. I stared at the hole in the arm of her jacket. Blood trickled out of it in pulses.

"Rose!" I fumbled with my seatbelt. "Rose!"

My hands were clumsy as I struggled. Where was my cell phone? Darkness whirled. I couldn't reach my back pocket. I struggled with the seat belt again. How could I save Rose?

I gave up and leaned back against the seat, my breath coming in gasps as I fought to control my panic. Through the spiderweb of cracks in the windshield, I saw a figure standing outside the car, watching us. Why didn't he help? The figure faded as darkness closed in.

Thirteen

E mma."
Rose's voice came from far away, as if I was underwater. I was floating underwater. I relaxed and sank down...

"Emma!"

I opened my eyes. The cracked windshield. The tree surrounded by the crumpled front end of the Range Rover. Rose.

"Emma, are you okay?"

Turning my head was all I needed to come fully aware. Rose's face was still bloody from a cut on her forehead. She held her hurt arm in her right hand.

"Yes, I think so." I unfastened my seat belt with fingers that finally obeyed my command. "But you - you're bleeding."

Her face was pale. "I've been shot, and we need help."

"Shot? How?" I stared at her upper arm. Blood soaked her sleeve.

"Emma." Her voice was firm. "We don't have time to worry about that now. We need help."

I looked into her eyes. She was in control as always. A thought flicked through my mind that this wasn't a new experience for her.

"What do I need to do?"

"Can you get out of the car?"

I tried to open my door, but it wouldn't budge. "Not this way."

"Then you'll have to kick out the windshield." She sucked in her breath. "But first, we need to stop this bleeding. There's a first aid kit in the back seat."

I turned in my seat and reached into the back. Strapped to the back of my seat was a small kit. I released the clasps and sat back down.

As I unzipped it, I asked, "What do we need?"

"Some gauze pads and something to tie them firmly onto the wound."

A tightness in her voice made me pause. "Rose, are you okay?"

"I'll be fine."

Together we worked to get the gauze pads in place. I tried not to look at the bloody hole, but Rose worked efficiently until all was set.

"What now?" I asked.

"I'll keep applying pressure," Rose said. "And we need that blanket I keep on the back seat."

I got the blanket and covered her with it.

"Now to call 9-1-1. Does your cell phone have a signal?"

I pulled it out of my back pocket. "No."

"Then you'll have to get to a place where you do." She took a deep breath. "And you'll need to do it quickly."

I remembered what Rose said about kicking out the windshield. It was laced with fine cracks, but the safety glass was still in one piece. The edge on my side was pulled away from the frame. I pressed against it with my hand, and it gave slightly. I shifted in my seat and put both feet against the window. One push folded it out of the way, and I climbed through the opening. Once I was on the ground, I looked back at Rose.

"I'm going to climb up to the road and see if I can get a signal there."

She nodded. "Be careful. The shooter is still out there."

I started climbing up the steep bank, following the torn path of destruction the Range Rover had made. I scanned the road bank far above and from side to side. Would I even see the shooter before he tried again? I paused to catch my breath.

Or had I already seen him? That figure I had seen through the windshield. It seemed like it had been hours ago. That shadow hadn't made a move to help us.

Grabbing a small tree that was still rooted in the side of the hill, I used it to pull myself up another few feet. Finally, I reached the road.

I gasped to catch my breath as I pulled my phone from my back pocket. One bar. I punched in the emergency number.

"Nine-One-One. What is your emergency?"

The connection was weak, causing the operator's voice to crackle. I gave her the information, hoping that she could understand, but before I was finished the call cut out. I checked my phone's screen. No bars.

I looked around. The road was cut into the side of a mountain, with the rise of the mountainside continuing up on the far side of the narrow ribbon of gravel. On my right, the road continued downhill. On my left, it climbed uphill and around a curve. I walked uphill on the road, keeping my screen active and watching for a signal. I was around the curve and almost out of sight of where we had gone off the road before I saw another bar. Then two. I called Cal.

"Hey, Emma. What's up?" I heard noise in the background. He was in his SUV.

"Someone shot Rose."

"What?" Urgency made his voice hard. "Where are you? Is she okay?"

"We're somewhere between Paragon and Rapid City. Rose was driving and the bullet hit her arm. We went off the road and hit a tree."

"What road are you on?"

I looked around at the unfamiliar landscape. "I don't know. Rose took a different way than Becky did last week."

"Is it a gravel road or paved?"

"Gravel. It goes along the side of a hill."

"I know right where you are. I'll be there in ten."

"I called nine-one-one, but I don't know if my call went through."

"I'll make sure they got the information." I heard his siren through the phone. "Stay safe, Emma."

I went back down the road to where I could see the Range Rover crumpled against the tree. Even though I longed to return to Rose, I knew I had to stay where I was so that Cal and the EMT's would see me. The Range Rover would be out of sight of anyone who drove by. I hugged my elbows and shivered. Ten minutes had never seemed so long.

Finally, I heard sirens in the distance. Cal was the first to arrive. He skidded to a halt, jumped out of the SUV and grabbed my upper arms. He looked into my eyes, then pulled me close.

"You look all right, thank the Lord." He held me at arm's length again. "You're sure you're not hurt? You have a pretty nasty cut."

I touched the aching spot on my forehead. I hadn't noticed the blood before now. "A little shook up. But Rose is still in the car. I have to get back to her now that you're here."

"Nope. You stay. The EMT's are on their way. I'll see to Rose."

He worked his way down the steep hill toward the Range Rover. When he reached it, he peered in the driver's side window, then turned to me with a thumbs up sign. My knees started quivering and I took a deep breath. She was okay.

Once the ambulance arrived, I let the EMT's take over. Someone sat me down on the back bumper of the emergency vehicle and wrapped a blanket around my shoulders.

"You'll be okay, hon," a middle-aged woman said. "Are you hurt anywhere other than the bump on your head?" I shook my head as she did a quick examination, including shining a flashlight into my eyes. "You just sit here and rest while we see to your friend."

"I have to watch." I shook off the blanket. "I'll go crazy just waiting here."

The paramedic frowned, then relented. "Okay. But don't try to go down into that gulch."

I stood at the edge of the road and watched the first responders pry the driver's side door open. They helped Rose out of the car, then strapped her into a rescue stretcher. After a few minutes, they brought her up the hill and I met them as they reached the top.

"Rose, are you okay?"

She smiled at me, but the corners of her mouth quivered. "I will be."

Cal grasped my arm and pulled me away. "You need to let the paramedics do their job."

"Is she really going to be okay?"

His grin was real, not a fake pasted on to make me feel better. "She's one tough lady."

"I had a thought that she has probably been shot before."

"So did I." He took my hand and led me back to the ambulance. "Have you been checked out?"

The paramedic that had helped me earlier tucked my blanket around my shoulders again. "I checked her, and everything appears normal. I'd still like to have her examined by the ER doctors in case that cut is more serious than it appears."

"That won't be necessary, will it?" I looked to Cal for help. "I feel fine, and I just want to go home."

"So that you can start figuring out who shot at you and Rose?"

I shifted my gaze to his shirt button. He knew me too well.

"I'll take responsibility for her," he said to the paramedic. "I'll bring her in if she shows any sign that she needs medical attention."

The paramedic took a computer tablet from the inside of the ambulance and typed a few things on it, then handed it to me. I signed the touch screen, then looked for Rose.

While we had been talking, the other paramedics had been attending to her and were now ready to put her into the ambulance.

I ignored the IV drip in her arm and the bandages on her bruised face. I only needed to see her eyes to know everything was going to be fine.

"Don't worry about me, dear," she said as the paramedics carried her stretcher past me. "They'll want to keep me in the hospital, but I haven't lost that much blood. I plan to be home by supper time. Have Montgomery bring you and Clara when he comes to pick me up and we'll get some pizza on the way home."

"Mrs. Blackwood," said a young man, "you're in no condition to be making supper plans."

I smiled at the young paramedic. "I think you're underestimating my aunt. If she says she's going to have pizza, then that's what we'll be doing."

Cal came up behind me as they closed the ambulance door. "I guess this means we'll be postponing our dinner arrangements for tonight."

The dinner date that wasn't a date. "I'm so sorry. With everything going on I had forgotten all about it."

"No problem." He looked very much the on-duty policeman with his sunglasses covering his eyes. "I'm going to be pretty busy for the rest of the day."

I nodded my understanding as I watched the busy crowd of police and paramedics around us.

"Do you want me to give you a ride home right away, or do you feel like taking a few minutes to reconstruct what happened while it's still fresh in your mind?"

"I want to figure out who tried to kill Rose. I'll stay as long as you need me."

"Tell me what happened."

"Rose was driving. We were talking about the inn. Then I heard a sound, like a stone had hit the car, and suddenly the Range Rover went off the road and hit that tree."

"Did you see or hear anything else?"

I shook my head. "It all happened so quickly. How did Rose get shot? There wasn't anyone around that I could see."

"The bullet went through the windshield and hit her left arm." Cal pointed to the debris trail of Rose's car. "There's where you went off the road, so somewhere in here is where the bullet made impact." He pointed to the road where we were standing.

"But that means the shooter was in front of us. Wouldn't we have seen him?"

"The bullet entered the windshield at a point higher than Rose's shoulder. He was probably somewhere on the slope above the road."

"Would there be any trace of him up there?"

"It depends on how much of a hurry he was in." Cal started along the road, winding through the other police cars and the tow truck that had arrived. "Look up the slope and see if you can find any place that looks like it's been disturbed recently."

We walked along the curve of the road as it traveled down the mountain, scanning the upper slope as we went. I didn't see anything, but suddenly Cal stopped.

"What is it?"

He nodded up the slope. "It looks like something is up there."

I followed him to a spot about twenty feet above the road. By the time I got there, my lungs were complaining from the exertion, but I didn't care. The ground was soft next to a large Ponderosa pine, and even I could see a well-defined footprint.

I looked down at the road. The place where we had been hit by the bullet was in a clear line of sight. I shivered and wrapped my jacket closer around me.

"Is this where he stood?"

"Not stood." He pointed to a deeper, rounded depression. "Knelt. He dropped to one knee, steadied himself against the tree, and took his shot."

He took a toothpick out of his shirt pocket and stuck it in the corner of his mouth.

I shuddered again. "He hit his target."

"No." Cal leveled his gaze at me. "If he had hit his target, Rose would be dead, and you would probably have been killed when the Range Rover went down into the gulch. But two things went wrong. He missed his aim, and that tree stopped the car from going all the way to the bottom."

He pointed at Rose's SUV far below us. Below it, the slope grew steeper and disappeared into a deep canyon. Feeling the same vertigo I had experienced at the overlook where Paul had been killed, I took a step back.

Cal started searching through the grayish brown pine needles and rotted pinecones surrounding the tree.

"What are you looking for?"

He brushed aside a clump of grass. "Anything that will give a clue about the shooter."

"What have you found out?"

The toothpick switched corners. "We are probably not dealing with a professional. He most likely used a bolt-action hunting rifle, and I would guess we're looking at a weekend hunter. Someone who has a rifle or access to one and decided to use it." He indicated the footprints. "He wasn't here very long before he took his shot, and he didn't stick around to see if the shot was successful."

My stomach flipped. "I just remembered. After the accident, I saw someone looking through the windshield at us."

Cal shot a look toward me. "Can you describe him?"

"He was just a shadow. The windshield was full of cracks. I blinked, and he was gone."

"Did he do anything?"

"He stood there, watching us. I couldn't figure out why he didn't help us."

"It was a man? You're sure it wasn't a woman?"

"Something about him seemed familiar, and yes, it was a man. He turned a little and bent at the waist..." My voice died off as I tried to place that familiar action.

"It's time to get you home. You look worn out."

"I am." My whole body ached, and I longed for a hot shower. "But what about the shooter? He's still out there somewhere."

"You let me worry about him."

He turned and grabbed my hand as we negotiated the slope down.

"But Cal, could it be the same person who murdered Dick, Paul, and Mary?"

He turned to look at me, his teeth clenched on the toothpick. "I'm sure of it."

The inn was quiet when we returned, but the peace didn't last long. Cal had just helped me up the stairs to my room when Becky burst in the front door and pounded up the steps.

"Emma?" She appeared at the door to my suite. "Are you alive? I heard you had been shot! Why aren't you in the hospital?"

Cal tucked a pillow behind my back. "Calm down. Emma is fine, but a little shaken up. I'd appreciate it if you'd stay with her for a while. I have work to do."

"Go back to work," I said, waving him out of the room. "Catch the bad guy."

Becky looked from me to Cal. "She wasn't shot?"

"She's fine. Rose is at the hospital with a minor wound-"

"Minor?" Becky's voice rose to a shriek.

"But Emma is okay."

"Yes, I'm just fine." I took the pillow from behind my back. "And I'd be a lot better if you two would stop talking about me as if I wasn't here."

Cal tipped the brim of his hat and left me with his nearly hysterical cousin.

"What can I do?" Becky asked. "Do you need some water? Something to eat?" She peered at the gauze bandage the paramedic had stuck to my forehead. "Your bandage looks okay. No bleeding."

"I'm fine." I reached up and pulled the gauze off, wincing as the tape tried its best to hold onto my skin. "I just want to get to the bottom of this. Rose and I were almost killed today.

"I'll get the clue board."

"First, would you go downstairs and get Thatcher from Rose's suite? The poor guy probably knows something is wrong."

In a few minutes we were set. I had changed to a clean outfit while Becky was downstairs, and Thatcher snuggled close to me on one side, while Tim settled into his usual spot on the back of the sofa. Becky sat on the other leg of the L and we both leaned over the clue board. I got a pad of sticky notes out of my bag.

"What are those for?"

"We're going to start eliminating suspects." I took one and put it over the women's names as I described the figure I had seen after the car hit the tree. "I know I saw a man, so that leaves out Clara, Nora, and Annie."

"I thought Annie and Roger left this morning."

"They did. But we can't assume they went home." I stuck another sticky note on the board. "And Rose isn't a suspect, since she was nearly a victim."

"So that leaves three." Becky pointed to Roger's name. "I think we can eliminate Roger anyway. He isn't the type to murder someone in cold blood."

I stuck a note over Roger's name. "I agree. That leaves just Sam and Montgomery."

"How do we decide which one it is?"

"We go through the clues again." I pointed to each one. "Sam keeps changing his story. First, he wants to investigate old mines, then it's casinos. I'm not sure what his game is."

"But that isn't suspicious, is it? And what would his motive be?"

"The motive." I rubbed Thatcher's ears as he whimpered in his sleep. "The notes Rose received make it sound like the motive centers around her past and the inn, but why?"

"What about Montgomery? Do any of the clues point to him?"

"Rose would be upset if she knew I had him on the suspect list. She trusts him completely, and they have a long history together."

"I know. They were both spies." Becky shivered. "Could it be that he's a double agent? Maybe the other side is paying him to get rid of Rose and make it look like it has nothing to do with espionage."

"Why do you think they were spies?"

"Oh, come on, Emma. This is small town life we're talking about here. Everyone knows about Rose's secret past. And Montgomery, with that British accent, has to be connected."

"You mean no one's secret past is secret?"

She grinned. "Of course not. But don't worry. We're all family here."

Becky laughed with me as I got up to get some water from the fridge. "Do you want some?" I asked, holding up the filtering pitcher.

"Sure."

I poured our drinks into a couple insulated tumblers and handed one to Becky. I took a drink while we stared at the clue board.

"Back to Sam." I took another drink as Thatcher rolled over. "Why is he here?"

"What was your nickname for him?"

"Seeker Sam, and his wife, Nosy Nora." I had almost forgotten about the mnemonics. "From the first moment I met them I thought they were looking for something."

"Maybe that's why he keeps changing. He's still looking for whatever it is."

"What about Nora? One minute they act like they're inseparable, and the next time I see them they're bickering."

"Like an old married couple." Becky finished the cliché.

I remembered their scene at breakfast that morning. "I wonder if the arguing could be an act."

"What do you mean?"

"Well, this is a weird idea, but maybe they aren't married, but are partners in crime instead."

"Why can't they be both?" Becky leaned forward. "A married pair of shrewd cat burglars."

The way she narrowed her eyes made me laugh. "Cat burglars? Be serious."

"Well, didn't Nora have some new jewelry? That Black Hills gold isn't cheap."

"Sam said he won at the casino and bought the jewelry for Nora. It could have happened that way, couldn't it?"

"You're right." Becky sighed and leaned back against the sofa. "And with the type of jewelry she has, we're talking hundreds of dollars, not thousands. Not a normal cat burglar target." She sat up again. "But could Sam have been the shadowy figure you saw?"

I closed my eyes, trying to recall exactly what I had seen. The memory was already fading. "The figure was tall and slim, so that could have been Sam." I popped my eyes open. "It also might have been Montgomery." I thought again. "But Montgomery has a military bearing, never slouches. This guy was more casual if that makes sense."

Becky took my pad of sticky notes and put one over Montgomery's name. We both stared at the lone remaining name.

"That's it then," Becky said. "Sam is the murderer."

"The classic method of elimination. Hercule Poirot would be proud of us."

But I couldn't celebrate. I had a feeling we were missing something.

"There's one problem," I said. "We don't have any evidence, and Cal can't arrest him without it."

"Then we need to find some."

"How?"

"You have a key to their room, don't you? And they're out for the day. It's just you and me here."

"Isn't Wil here?"

"I saw him driving toward Rapid in his Prius earlier this morning, right after breakfast."

"There must be another way to find the evidence." I stalled for time. Something didn't feel right about this. "And we can't just search their room. It's trespassing, and any evidence we did find wouldn't be admissible in court."

"You watch too many cop shows on television. Private detectives do it all the time."

"Now who has been watching too much television?" I rubbed my temple. "Besides, without knowing what Sam might be doing and why, we wouldn't have any idea what to look for. We need to find his motive first. Why would he kill three people, and try to kill two more? What is in it for him?"

My headache was getting worse. I got some pain medicine out of my bag and took two of the pills.

"The inn?" Becky shrugged.

"Maybe. But even if he killed all of us, what would be the reason?" I shook my head. "It has to be something more."

"Could he be working for someone else?"

"You mean like a hit man?"

"Yeah. I could see him as the gangster type."

"Now you're grasping at straws." I yawned. Now that I was at home and safe, I couldn't stay awake.

"I'm going to get out of here so you can rest." Becky stood and slid the clue board back under the sofa. "I'll check on you in a couple hours, okay?"

"That sounds good." I kicked my shoes off and tucked them under the ottoman.

I didn't even hear the door click closed as I pulled Thatcher toward me and cuddled with him. My brain swirled with different images. Rose's pale face. The shadowy figure through the shattered safety glass of the windshield. Mary stumbling down the stairs. Paul's red scarf at the bottom of the ravine. The piece of uranium ore that had been clenched in Paul's hand.

Uranium. Hadn't someone mentioned uranium last week? The night everyone had arrived at the inn?

Thatcher groaned in his sleep.

Rose had spoken against uranium mining...what had Sam said?

"With a rich uranium strike you could make millions."

Some people would consider that amount of money worth killing for. But would Sam? I sighed and hugged Thatcher closer and fell asleep dreaming of gangsters and radioactive rocks.

A knock at my door sent Thatcher into a barking frenzy as he jumped off the sofa. I sat up and rubbed my face. The light outside had changed to a soft blue. I must have been asleep for an hour or more.

"Hush, Thatcher." I grabbed his collar and opened the door.

"Oh." Wil arched his eyebrows as he stared at me. "You're all right."

"I'm okay. Just a little tired." I pulled Thatcher out of the way. "I've got to have some water. Do you want anything?"

"No, thanks." He closed the door behind him as he stepped into the room, and I let go of Thatcher's collar. The dog glared at Wil as he jumped back onto the sofa.

"Do you have any updates on Rose? I've been asleep for a while." I picked up the tumbler from the floor and drained it.

"Yeah. Cal called and asked me to check up on you, since he said you had been injured, too." He peered at the bump on my head. "He said Rose is fine and will be home for supper. They're bringing pizza."

I grinned. "I told that paramedic he was underestimating Rose when he said she'd probably be at the hospital overnight."

"What happened, anyway?" Wil took my spot on the sofa and crossed an ankle over his knee.

"Didn't you hear? Someone shot at us while we were on our way into Rapid City." I went to the kitchen for more water.

"I only heard that Rose was at the hospital. Was she badly hurt?"

I sat down on the sectional again. "The bullet wounded her arm, and the car went off the road." I shivered, thinking about our close call. "If we hadn't hit a tree, we would have plunged into a canyon."

"Both of you should be dead," Wil said, his voice holding just a bit of his usual complaining tone.

"But we're not. Sorry to disappoint you." I took another drink.

He laughed. "I didn't mean anything. Just that it sounds like that tree saved your lives."

"Yeah. Rose is surprisingly tough for her age."

"That's for sure." He stood up.

"Are you going to have pizza with us?" At the thought of food, my stomach growled. I had missed lunch.

"I thought you had other plans."

My non-date with Cal. The reason I had given to turn Wil down when he had asked me out.

"The accident changed things. I don't think I should be going out tonight."

"My offer still stands, in case you don't feel like spending the evening with the ancient ones."

I laughed at the face he made, as if spending time with Clara, Montgomery, and Rose was as distasteful as eating a sour pickle.

"I enjoy being around them. I'm glad Clara and Montgomery are both staying another week."

His face turned dark, the sour expression lingering. "It's your funeral," he said, then walked out the door.

I didn't care what Becky said. That guy gave me the creeps.

Fourteen

By morning I was beginning to feel normal again and ready for a cup of Wil's coffee. But as soon as I started down the stairs, I knew I was out of luck. No delicious rich coffee smell wafted from the kitchen.

I swung open the kitchen door. "Wil, you know I need my coffee in the morning."

The room was dark. No Wil. I switched on the lights. The empty pizza box from last night still sat on the counter near the trash can, waiting to be taken out to the dumpster. No one had been in the kitchen since last night's supper.

"Wil." I heard the growl of disgust in my voice. He knew we still had guests. How could he oversleep?

Grabbing the pizza box, I took it out to the dumpster. On my way back through the garage I stopped at the bottom of the stairs leading to Wil's apartment. His Prius was in its parking place, so he must be at home.

I put my foot on the first step. Did I want to confront him about this? I chewed my bottom lip, then stopped myself. It didn't matter how creepy the guy was, he needed to show up for work on time. I ran up the steps and knocked on the door.

Nothing.

I pounded.

Still nothing.

I tried the lever and the door swung open. The kitchen and living room were dark, but enough light emanated from the microwave clock to see that the bedroom door on the opposite side of the apartment was open. Was he in bed? Probably.

"Wil?" No answer. I tried again. "Wil?"

I closed the door on the silent apartment and went back down the stairs. There was no way I was going to walk into Wil's bedroom to wake him up. Not me. If he didn't show up for work, I'd let Rose decide how to handle it.

But when I walked back into the kitchen, it hit me. Breakfast. I checked my watch. Almost six o'clock. I opened the refrigerator, hoping Wil had prepped something, but it was nearly empty. A couple dozen eggs. Some butter. I checked the freezer and found a container of Becky's muffins. I set it on the counter to start thawing.

Coffee. I needed coffee, and it was past time to start the pot brewing in the dining room.

After turning on the coffee maker, I began the routine of setting up the dining room for breakfast, all the time calling Wil names in my mind. Only a stuck up, overconfident person wouldn't tell someone if he wasn't going to show up for work. He didn't even have a menu posted so someone could step in for him if he was sick.

Menu. Maybe it was on his laptop. I went into the kitchen and checked the drawer where he kept the computer, but it was empty. I groaned and leaned against the counter.

"Emma?" Montgomery had opened the kitchen door. "Is everything all right?"

If Wil showed up right now, I'd kill him for putting me in this position in front of a guest.

I forced a smile. "Yes, of course. Everything is fine."

He stepped into the kitchen. "Emma, my dear, I can tell when someone is skirting the truth. You're upset."

In normal circumstances, I would confide in Rose concerning Wil's actions, but the past few days had been far from normal.

"Okay. You're right. Wil didn't show up for work this morning and there is no breakfast for you and the other guests."

He smiled at me, his mustache twitching. "No problem. We can make our own meal."

"Maybe you can, but I know nothing about cooking."

His chuckle took my stress level down a few notches.

"What do we have to work with?"

I opened the cooler. "Some eggs and butter. I pulled today's muffins out of the freezer, so once they're thawed, we can have those. But there is no way we can put on one of Wil's fabulous meals."

"We don't have to." Montgomery took his sports jacket off and put on one of Wil's chef aprons. "A simple breakfast will do just fine. Eggs made to order, muffins, and coffee. Is there any juice in the pantry?"

"I'll check." I paused, then stood on my toes to give Montgomery a peck on the cheek. "Thank you. You're a life saver. I can see why Rose depends on you."

He blushed. Actually blushed. Then he turned and started opening cupboard doors as if his life depended on finding out what was kept in each one.

Montgomery was the perfect cook. He kept up an amusing banter from the kitchen as he made eggs to order for each of us, making Rose and Clara laugh. Sam even smiled at his antics.

Nora was the only problem.

"Where is Wil?" she asked, poking her fork at the scrambled eggs Montgomery had cooked for her.

I exchanged glances with Rose. I had let her know about Wil's absence, but we hadn't had a chance to discuss what to do about it.

"He didn't show up this morning," I said as I refilled her coffee cup. "I'm sure he has a good explanation. But meanwhile, we're grateful to Montgomery for filling in for him."

"I hope you'll be removing the cost of this meal from our bill," she said, pushing her plate away.

"Shut your yap, Nora," Sam said as he held his cup out for a refill. "Breakfast is fine. It's time to get going."

"What are your plans for today?" asked Rose.

Sam and Nora exchanged glances.

"Some exploring, I guess you could say." Sam shoved his chair back as he stood. "Maybe a little treasure hunting."

"Have fun," Rose said.

Sam and Nora went upstairs to their room. I started clearing the tables, but Clara shooed me away. "If Montgomery is doing the cooking, the least I can do is take care of this while you get ready for church. You and Rose are both knackered from yesterday and deserve a wee bit of pampering."

"If you say so..." I hesitated.

"Go." She gave me a light shove toward the stairs. "I'll have this done in two shakes of a lamb's tail."

I obeyed and ran up the stairs. For one thing, I had to see where Sam and Nora were going, and my bedroom window gave me a great view of the driveway.

Tim meowed and jumped off the sofa to greet me. I picked him up, scratching his ears as I peered out my bedroom window, standing to one side so I wouldn't be seen. After a few minutes, I saw the Nelsons' sedan make its way down the drive to Graves' Gulch Road. Without stopping, the car turned left.

Up into the Hills. Toward the mine.

I set Tim on the bed and grabbed a jacket from my closet. I had to follow them. Sam had tried to make it sound like their exploring and treasure hunting was a whim, but that glance he and Nora had exchanged warned me that their plans for today might be more serious.

Starting back down the steps, I paused at the landing. Rose was sitting at her table with Montgomery while the sounds of Clara loading the dishwasher emanated from the kitchen. What excuse could I give for heading out the door an hour before church?

Thatcher's bark from Rose's apartment gave me the answer.

I smiled at Rose and Montgomery. "I thought I heard Thatcher whining. I'll take him for his walk this morning."

"Thank you," Rose said. "He needs more exercise than I can give him today."

Rose's door was unlocked, and the corgi was waiting in his crate. He wiggled all over when he saw me.

"Are you ready for your walk?" I took the leash of its hook next to the door, carrying it with me in case Thatcher wasn't cooperative.

He was ready. The dog didn't pause until he reached his favorite post next to the driveway. Two more stops and some sniffing later, we were on Graves' Gulch Road.

"Okay, buddy. You've gotten your business done and now it's time to get some exercise."

Once I turned toward the mine, Thatcher was with me all the way up the hill. By the time I reached the Forest Service gate and the Nelsons' parked car, I was out of breath. Thatcher sniffed at the car's wheels while I searched for a sign of where they had gone.

There were only two choices: through the gate into the forest, or on the trail leading to the mine. I checked the dusty road looking for any footprints, but the scuff marks didn't tell me anything. The same with the trail leading to the mine.

I looked at Thatcher. "Well, buddy? Where do you think they went?"

He wagged his tail and started up the trail toward the mine, sniffing the ground as he went. I let him take the lead. He took me past the mine, then off the trail and down the hill toward the inn below us, winding his way around trees and shrubs. He stopped near a small rock outcropping and sniffed the ground carefully, his shiny black nose quivering.

"Did you find something?"

More sniffing. I examined the ground but didn't see anything. Then I noticed some loose rocks below the outcropping. I picked up one that was nearly as big as Thatcher's head. Pink threaded through the whitish rock. Was this rose quartz?

I turned the rock over. One end was sharp and fragmented. Dirt and pine needles were lodged into the rough stone. I looked closer. A few strands of hair were embedded in the dirt. I dropped the stone.

My stomach queasy, I scanned the trees around us, hoping I could find this spot again. Cal needed to see that rock before something happened to it. It had to be the murder weapon in Dick's death. I looked back at the space under the rock outcropping. In my imagination I could almost see poor Dead Dick, kneeling next to the rocks, examining something. But then the murderer - Sam - creeps up behind him, grabs that piece of rose quartz, and bashes his head in.

I shuddered and backed away from the scene. Where was Sam? And Nora? I spun around, certain that they were sneaking up behind me. Nothing.

Thatcher yipped. He did a corgi stomp, pounding on the ground with both front feet, then nosed something in a tangle of grass. I knelt next to him. It was a cell phone.

Definitely something else to show Cal. But what if Sam and Nora were watching us? I didn't dare turn around, but I couldn't leave the cell phone here. But how could I take it to Cal without destroying any fingerprints that might be on it?

I was about to ask Thatcher, but then stopped. Talking to a dog? Was I going crazy? Maybe just a little, because the sight of his grinning face reminded me of the doggy-doo bags in the holder clipped to his leash.

"Thanks, pup. That will be perfect."

Before I bagged the phone, I took out my own and took pictures of it and the area. I even went back and snapped a picture of the rose quartz, just in case. Then we started back to the inn.

By the time we got back to the Sweetbrier, Rose was ready for church and waiting for me. Church! In my time up at the mine, I had forgotten that today was Sunday. It took me less than five minutes to change and join the others in Montgomery's rented car. Even so, we were late. Church had already started when the four of us slipped into seats in the back row.

All through the service, the knowledge of that cell phone waiting in my purse distracted me and it seemed like Pastor Charlie gave the longest sermon ever. I watched the back of Cal's head as he sat near the front. Would he be able to identify whose phone I had found? It had to be Dick's, and he must have lost it on the day he was murdered.

But then it could be someone else's. People lost cell phones all the time, right? I tried to focus on the sermon even though I knew that people didn't lose their cell phones in the middle of a forest, several yards away from any trail or road.

When the last hymn was sung and the benediction over, Rose, Clara, and Montgomery were ready to go back to the inn. The pinched lines around Rose's eyes showed that she was still recovering from our experience of the day before.

"We can wait for you," she said when I explained I wanted to talk to Cal.

"Don't. You need to get home and get some rest. I'll walk back to the inn."

After they left, I made my way toward Cal. The boys surrounded him.

"This week, Cal?" one of them asked. From the cowlick, I guessed that he was Jeremy. "You promised you'd take us camping soon."

"Don't you have school this week?"

A younger boy grinned. "Maybe we have spring break."

"And maybe you had spring break last month." Cal rubbed the boy's buzz haircut. "We will go camping, but you know the rules. Not on a school night, and not while I'm on a case."

A couple of the boys groaned. Cal glanced up and saw me watching.

"I might be able to get away on Friday, so we'll try to plan for that. You guys see if that will work for your dads, okay?"

The boys ran toward the door and Cal turned to me. "Hey. What's up?"

"Does something have to be up?"

The corners of his mouth twitched. "It usually is when you're around."

"I found this when I was walking Thatcher." I pulled the doggy poo bag out of my purse.

Cal cleared his throat.

"It isn't what you think." I unrolled the bag and opened it to show him the cell phone inside.

"Where did you find this?"

"Near the mine, but off the trail a little." I opened the photo files on my phone. "And this rock. It has to be the murder weapon."

Cal scrolled through the photos I had taken. "You took these this morning?"

"Yes."

"Come show me," he said as he started toward the door. "It might be important."

"That's what I thought," I said, walking as fast as I could to keep up with his long strides. "And there's more."

He opened the passenger door of his SUV for me. "Tell me on the way to the mine." He looked up toward the sky. "We need to get up there before it starts raining."

I glanced at the gathering clouds and jumped into the vehicle. Cal got in, started the engine, and made his way to the main road.

"You said you had more?" he asked as he turned onto the paved road.

"I know who the murderer is. Or are."

Cal made the turn onto Graves' Gulch Road. "Who?"

"Sam and Nora Nelson. Or maybe only one of them, but the other one is involved, too."

"What makes you think it's them?"

"Process of elimination." We passed the inn and headed up toward the mine. "We considered each of the suspects, and the only one it could be is Sam."

"We?"

"Becky and I."

Cal parked the car next to the Forest Service gate and looked at me. "I should have known."

"Becky and I have good ideas."

"Sometimes. But I know my cousin." He opened the door and got out. "She has an active imagination."

I got out of the SUV. "I've been accused of the same thing. But I didn't imagine the cell phone and this rock."

He opened the back door and grabbed his duffel bag. "Lead the way."

I followed the trail past the mine, looking for the spot where Thatcher had led me down the hill.

"I think this is the spot."

"You aren't sure?"

The wind picked up, dropping the temperature a notch. Then I saw the small outcropping. "I'm sure."

"Which rock did you think was the murder weapon?"

There were several rocks scattered on the ground. I picked up the nearest one, but there was no rough end. No hairs caught between the layers. I tried the next one, and then the next.

"I know it was here this morning." I scrolled though the pictures on my phone. "See? These rocks are still here, but not this one."

Cal peered at the photo, then compared it with the real thing. "You're right. One is missing. You know what this means." Cal pulled a toothpick from his shirt pocket. "The murderer saw you this morning and knows you found the murder weapon, if that's what it was."

"It had to be!" My voice squeaked. Then the weight of what Cal had said hit me. "Sam and Nora were here. I followed them. They must have been watching me, and then took the rock after Thatcher and I left."

Cal stuck the toothpick in the corner of his mouth. "Whether it was the Nelsons or not remains to be seen. But one thing is clear." He frowned at me. "You are not to go anywhere alone until we catch this guy. I don't think you realize the danger you were in this morning."

I frowned back. "How can I catch them if I don't go anywhere?"

"You leave that up to me." A few raindrops started falling. "We need to get out of here before it starts raining in earnest. But first, show me where you found the cell phone."

The spot was only a few yards away. Cal examined the tuft of grass where I had found it, then pointed to an area where the stones gave way to dirt.

"Do you see those tracks?"

Two narrow wheel tracks pointed toward the inn. "What are they? Bicycle tires?"

"More like a cart of some kind."

I remembered the strange cart hanging on the garage wall. "Like a game cart?"

"Exactly like a game cart."

"Wil has one in the garage at the inn. Do you think Sam used it to transport Dick's body when he planted it in my room?"

"It could be." He took a camera out of his duffel and started snapping pictures just as I felt a raindrop. Finally, he stood up. "This rain is going to wash away a lot of evidence." I had never heard such reluctance in his voice.

"It can't be helped, can it?"

"Nope. Let's get back to the inn."

He grabbed my arm and started up the hill toward the trail. As we hurried past the rock outcropping, something caught my eye.

"Wait." I stopped and looked closer at one side of the rough rock. "Isn't this some of that calico quartz? The kind that might be uranium?"

The raindrops grew heavier, but Cal pulled some brush away to examine the rock face.

"You're right."

"Then this is where poor Dick Brill was killed. He probably stopped here to examine the rock, and the murderer crept up behind him…" I didn't want to go on.

Cal snapped some photos of the cliff and the ground at its base, but then the rain started pouring in sheets. We ran for the SUV and climbed inside.

Cal said something, but the noise of the rain on the roof was so loud I couldn't hear him.

"What?"

He leaned close to my ear. "We'll need to stay put until the worst is over."

I nodded my head and settled in to watch the rain. In between the sluices of water running down the windshield, I realized that something was missing.

"The Nelsons' car," I said.

"What?" Cal leaned closer to me again.

"The Nelsons' car isn't here. It was this morning."

The toothpick bobbed up and down as Cal chewed on it. I crossed my arms to try to keep warm in my damp clothes and felt like chewing on a toothpick myself. Had Sam and Nora been watching Thatcher and me this morning? They must have. That's how they knew I had found the piece of rose quartz. The murder weapon.

I shivered. I could have been their next victim, which brought another question. Why wasn't I?

Finally, the rain lessened to a shower and Cal started the car and drove to the inn.

The Nelsons' car was in the parking lot, making my stomach sink. Knowing what I knew, how could

I face them? How could I pretend to be a welcoming hostess to them when I knew they were murderers?

I glanced at Cal's profile as he parked the SUV. Maybe I wouldn't have to.

"Sam and Nora's car is here. Are you going to arrest them?"

Cal turned off the engine and faced me. "On what grounds?"

"They are the murderers. I know they are."

"What evidence do you have?"

"They have the murder weapon. You saw that it was missing."

"Someone has the murder weapon, but we don't know that Sam and Nora do."

"You could search their room for it. Get a warrant."

The toothpick bobbed up and down. "Even if I was able to get a warrant with nothing more than your intuition and circumstantial evidence to go on, why would they bring the rock back to their room? Why wouldn't they just pitch it somewhere in the forest?" He opened his door. "Sorry, Emma. Without solid evidence, I can't do anything except keep investigating."

I followed him to the front of the inn where he held the door open for me. The rain had let up, leaving only stray drops falling from the ceiling of pine branches above.

"Don't say anything to the Nelsons about what you suspect," he said.

Through the open door, I could see Sam and Nora in the dining room, talking with Rose and Clara.

"Maybe I could force them to admit something." I wasn't sure how I would do that, but it was worth a try.

"Nope. Don't do it. Don't even mention the case. If they are guilty, any suspicion that you might be on to them could make them clam up. They'd leave the area and we'd never be able to bring them in." The toothpick shifted to the other corner of his mouth. "If they're guilty, that is."

"If? Who else can it be?"

His face was stony as I walked past him and into the inn. I put a smile on my face and greeted the group with nods. Montgomery waved from the kitchen where he was stirring a pitcher of lemonade.

"Did you and Cal have a good talk?" Rose asked.

Cal had stalked in behind me and sat at a table near the others. Close enough to hear the conversation, but far enough away to be outside the group.

"Yes, we did. He was able to answer some questions I had, and then we went up to the mine to look around."

I focused on Sam's face as I said this, but he didn't react.

Clara patted the chair next to hers. "Monty is making some lemonade. Why don't you sit and join us?"

I took the seat between Clara and Nora, my back to Cal. "Did you have a good morning?" I asked Nora. "I hope the rain didn't ruin your plans."

She blushed, then laughed. "Oh, no. We were back here before it started raining."

Montgomery set glasses on the table, then filled them with fresh lemonade from the pitcher. I pulled one of the glasses toward me.

"What did the two of you do today?" I asked as I ran my thumb through a bit of condensation on the outside of the glass. "You went up to the mine, didn't you?"

Behind me, Cal cleared his throat. I ignored him.

Sam laughed, grabbed one of the glasses and took a long drink. "What makes you think we went up to the mine?" he asked after he set his glass down. "Why would we bother with that old place?"

I heard Cal's warning tone behind me. "Emma..."

"I saw you head that way in your car this morning. I thought maybe you went for a hike in the forest."

Sam frowned, but Nora laughed. "Hiking? Us?"

I shrugged, waiting to hear what Sam had to say.

"Listen, young lady," he said, poking his finger toward me. "What we do and where we go isn't any of your business." He stood up, his chair protesting as he shoved it back.

"She didn't mean anything," Rose said, jumping into the conversation. "Although perhaps Emma could have been a bit more tactful." She gave me a sideways look that I read as, *You had better make this right.*

I forced my voice into a civil tone. "I'm sorry."

Although I wasn't. I wasn't sorry about anything I said to a murderer, but his defensive attitude was as good as a confession to me.

"Can I refill your lemonade for you?" I went to get the pitcher from the counter as Sam relaxed and sat in his chair again.

I filled Sam's glass and made the rounds of the table.

"Maybe you were right, Nora," Sam said. "Maybe it is time to go home."

"But what about-" Nora broke off and blushed when she noticed all of us were listening. She cleared her throat and started over. "Didn't you have a project you wanted to finish?"

"Do stay," Rose said, her voice as gracious and welcoming as always. "I would hate to see you leave now, just when you were so pleased that you were able to continue staying in the Dublin Bay. That room is perfect for you."

Sam scanned the faces around the table, avoiding both Cal and me.

"We'll stay until next Friday."

He shifted in his seat and stirred some sugar into his lemonade. His gaze then fell on me, staring as I returned to my seat. The conversation continued as Clara mentioned the weather and Sam's gaze went back to his glass.

Another week with a murderer at the inn? Cal had better find some evidence to incriminate this pair soon.

Fifteen

The sun was setting by the time Sam and Nora left the inn. They didn't share their supper plans as they stalked out the door, although it seemed to me that Nora shot a guilty look toward Rose as she sat in the dining room with Clara and Montgomery.

The three of them were chatting with Cal. I heard a few words. "Quartz." "Mine." "Emma." Enough to know they were talking about the case. And me.

I was cleaning the coffee machine, getting it ready for the next morning when the phone at the reception desk rang. Before I could dry my hands, Rose had answered it. From her end of the conversation, it sounded like someone was calling about reservations for next week. The inn wouldn't be empty after all. With Montgomery and Clara both staying on, plus the possibility of more guests, we wouldn't feel the absence of the Nelsons so strongly.

Once Cal finally decided he had enough evidence to arrest them.

I finished up my work and joined the others around the table just as Rose hung up the phone.

"That was a reservation for next week, a family of four." Rose didn't sit down but stood behind the chair she had been occupying.

"We'll put them in the Snow Goose and the Albertine, then?" I asked. "The adjoining suites?"

"If Cal is done investigating in those rooms." Rose grimaced and rolled her shoulder, evidence that her wound was bothering her. "They specifically asked if this was the inn where Paul Peterson had been staying when he died. It sounds like they might be fans. They plan to arrive on Tuesday afternoon and stay through Saturday."

Cal stood, picking up his hat from the table. "I've finished my investigations in those rooms, so yes, they're available." He slid the cowboy hat onto his curly hair. "I'm off, but I'll keep you updated on the case."

"I'm on my way to an early bedtime," Rose said as she started toward her suite. But then she stopped and turned back toward us. "By the way, has anyone seen Wil this weekend? He usually checks in with me on Sunday evening to make plans for the week, but I haven't heard from him."

"He wasn't here for breakfast this morning," Montgomery said.

Clara set her teacup in its saucer. "I often hear him in the kitchen during the day, but I haven't today, and I don't think I did yesterday, either."

Rose looked at me. "Have you seen him?"

"I went to wake him up when he didn't show up for breakfast this morning, but he must have been

237

dead to the world. He didn't hear me knock. I opened his door, but the apartment was dark and quiet."

"Did you see him?" Cal asked.

"No. I didn't go into his bedroom."

We all stared at each other.

Cal put his hat back on the table. "When was the last time anyone saw him?"

"I talked to him yesterday afternoon, but surely someone has seen him since then." I couldn't stop the cold feeling of dread that filled my stomach.

Clara shook her head, and Montgomery did the same.

"Then he's missing." Rose sank into her chair. "Where can he be?"

"Is his car here?" Cal asked.

"It was in the garage this morning." I rubbed my cold fingers. "You don't think he could be another one, do you?"

"Another victim?" Cal took a toothpick from his shirt pocket. "We need to find out if he's really missing before we jump to conclusions." He stuck the toothpick in his mouth. "Emma, please come with me."

I followed Cal down the hall to the garage, turning on the light as we entered. Yes, Wil's Prius was still in its place.

"What now?" I asked.

Cal didn't answer but led the way to the stairs and up to Wil's apartment.

I followed slowly. "Don't you need a warrant?"

"Not when I have probable cause that a crime has been committed."

"Then you think he has been murdered, too?"

He reached the top of the steps and looked back at me. "Just give me a hand here. Let me know if Wil's apartment looks the same as it did this morning."

As the door swung open at Cal's touch, I stepped in. The blinds were drawn, and the room was bathed in a twilight glow. "Everything is the same." I kept my voice to a whisper. Wil must be in the next room.

Cal crossed the living room and went through the open bedroom door, pulling his flashlight from his belt and switching it on. I heard him go into the bathroom, then back to the bedroom. He came out to the living room, shining his light over the furniture and walls as he came toward me.

"No sign that he's been here in the last twenty-four hours."

"Isn't that pretty specific? How can you tell?"

He ran his hand along the kitchen island. "Little things. The towels in the bathroom are dry, and his bed is unmade."

"Maybe he's just messy."

Cal lifted one eyebrow. "Or that he's a guy who lives alone." He checked his hand. "And the dust on the counter hasn't been disturbed."

"That tells you he hasn't been here for a day?"

"We live in a semi-arid climate. Things get dusty in a matter of hours." He waved toward the gun safe in the corner of the room. "Has Wil mentioned his guns to you?"

"Rose said he likes to go deer hunting, but Wil hasn't said anything."

Cal walked over to the small safe and pulled the door open.

"It wasn't locked?" I asked as I joined him and peeked inside.

"That's what caught my attention."

"His gun is still there." A long gun stood upright in the corner of the safe while small boxes lined the top shelf.

"That's a shotgun." Cal shined the flashlight on the gun. "A twenty-gauge, a popular size for hunting pheasants and small game." He let the beam play on the labels of the boxes. "Plenty of shotgun shells here, and also ammunition for a rifle, but his hunting rifle isn't here."

"Could Sam have stolen it?"

"When I asked Wil if he owned a rifle, he said he did, but that it was at a friend's house in Minnesota. He said he left it there when he went hunting last winter."

"You sound like you didn't believe him."

"Wil likes to show off his possessions. I don't see him leaving a gun like that anywhere." He focused the flashlight beams on another set of boxes. "Now this is interesting. This is ammunition for a nine-millimeter handgun, but there isn't one here."

"Sam took Wil's pistol, too?"

"Or Wil took it with him when he left. Either way, we can assume that our suspect is armed, either with a hunting rifle, or with Wil's nine mil."

"What's our next step? Report him as a missing person?"

Cal tapped the badge on his belt. "We already have. I'll set the crew to work tracing his credit cards and phone. If nothing turns up there, I'll bring the search and rescue team up tomorrow to start combing the forest."

"Tomorrow?" My voice squeaked as it always did when I was upset. "You know the Nelsons have already killed him. We should go up to the mine and start looking for his body now. And you need to arrest Sam and Nora before anyone else dies."

I drew a breath to continue but Cal stopped me. "Emma, who is the deputy here?"

That deflated me. "You are. You're the one with the badge."

"And the gun."

"And the gun," I repeated.

"And what did I ask you to do?"

His voice had dropped as he stepped closer and encircled me in his arms. I could almost describe it as tender. Was he worried about me?

"You asked me to never go anywhere alone."

I leaned into him as he held me close. His uniform smelled like Old Spice and French fries. An odd combination.

"You have to be careful. You're a target for this murderer for some reason, you and Rose both." He lifted his hands to my shoulders and held me at arm's length. "Promise me that you won't go searching for Wil by yourself." He cleared his throat. "Or with Becky."

I held up one hand in a mock Boy Scout salute. "On my honor." I lowered my hand. "Unless-"

"Unless nothing." He frowned. "I guess I'll have to take that as a yes."

"Okay." I swallowed, thinking of all the possibilities that could come up before tomorrow's search. "But what if-"

"No what-ifs. You need to stay safe. Let me handle the dangerous stuff."

How naive did he think I was? I had faced danger before. I didn't like it, but I could do it. I was just about to tell him that I could handle whatever Sam and Nora could dish out when he motioned for me to go down the stairs while he locked the door.

In the dining room, Cal told Rose and the others that he was treating Wil as a missing person.

"I was afraid you wouldn't find him," said Rose. "I called Becky and asked her to cook breakfast for our guests tomorrow."

"What about her baking?" I asked.

"She'll be able to do that here, and then transport the items down to the café. She seemed excited to use Wil's kitchen, even though she said she was worried about him."

Poor Becky. What if Wil really was the next victim? She still had a first-class crush on the guy even though he had given her no reason to hope there was a future for them.

Cal left and Rose went to bed. Clara and Montgomery made their way to their respective rooms while I cleared the table and straightened the chairs. I was loading the dishwasher when I heard a commotion from the entryway. Thumping and banging, followed by the door slamming. What in the world?

Remembering my earlier run-in with intruders, I pushed the kitchen door open a couple inches and peered out. I caught a flash of a black ponytail and scooted down the short hall as fast as I could before Becky made any more noise.

"What are you doing?" I asked, grabbing a bag before it hit the floor.

"Hey, girl." Becky dropped a large duffel bag from her other hand that clanged when it hit the floor. "I thought I'd bring my stuff up here and get an early start on tomorrow's breakfast."

"You didn't need to bring your entire kitchen, did you?"

Becky surveyed the bags surrounding her on the floor and shrugged. "A girl needs her own tools, you know."

I threaded one hand through the straps of three more duffel bags.

"Let's get these into the kitchen. Rose has already gone to bed and we don't want to wake her."

Becky picked up the rest of the bags and followed me to Wil's domain.

"How is she doing? She looked kind of worn out at church this morning."

"I know. I think it bothers her that she didn't spring back from the shooting as quickly as she thought she should." I grinned. "But other than being tired, she only has a bit of pain and stiffness. Not bad for what she went through."

"How many do we have for breakfast tomorrow?" Becky started unpacking her duffel bags.

"The Nelsons, Clara, Montgomery, and Rose. Plus, you and I, of course." I grabbed a nested stack of muffin pans out of a bag. "Are you going to be able to do all of your baking here, plus breakfast for the inn?"

"No problem." She set a handful of stainless-steel whisks on the counter. "But what about Wil? Rose said he might be missing. Are you sure he didn't take a few days off and forgot to tell anyone?"

"I'm sure, and Cal is convinced. Besides, his car is still in the garage."

"And no one has seen him since yesterday?"

I shook my head as her eyes grew shiny with moisture.

"You don't think he's-" She grabbed a paper towel from the holder by the sink and blew her nose. "He can't be another victim of the murderer. He just can't be."

I put one arm around her shoulder. "Don't worry. We'll find him."

"How?"

"Cal is bringing a search and rescue team tomorrow morning."

Becky sniffed. "I guess we'll just have to wait and see if they find him and pray that he's still alive."

As we finished unpacking the rest of Becky's gear, I silently regretted my promise to Cal. He wouldn't get here with the search team until midmorning or later. Becky and I could have started searching at first light.

I picked up a fluted tart pan with a removable bottom and set it on the counter. I took the bottom out, then set it back in. Ingenious. Somehow, I'd have to be just as ingenious to search for Wil in the morning and still keep the promise I kind-of made to Cal.

I slept that night, even though I never thought I would be able to relax enough to stay in bed.

Becky slept in the Westerland since it was empty until the next guests came.

"I could crash on your couch," she had said. "It's only for a few hours."

I had groaned as I checked my watch. It was already after midnight, and I had spent the last few hours helping Becky mix dough, chop veggies for the baked omelet she was making for breakfast and gossiping. It had been way too many years since I had enjoyed so much girl time and I had lost track of how late the night was growing.

When my alarm went off, I already felt the effects of my night owl ways. I took a quick shower then headed downstairs to give Becky a hand with breakfast. The warm, yeasty fragrance of fresh-baked bread greeted me as I swung open the kitchen door. Six loaves were on cooling racks on the prep counter.

"Hey, girl," Becky greeted me.

She poured a cup of coffee and handed it to me. I inhaled the rich fragrance.

"Wil must have returned." I took another deep breath, feeling the caffeine start working before I even took a sip.

"Nope." Becky turned back to the fruit salad she was stirring. "I found his stash. He buys Dark Canyon, their Rattlesnake Brew. It's a local coffee company."

I took a sip. "And he had me convinced it was some exotic gourmet blend."

She grinned at me as she dumped a pile of fresh blueberries into the bowl. "Just because it's local doesn't mean it isn't exotic or gourmet."

"This is definitely what we'll be serving in the dining room from now on." I took another swallow, then reluctantly put the coffee cup down on the end of the counter. "I have a few minutes. What can I do to help?"

Becky set me to work mixing a batch of muffins while she pulled a sheet tray full of hamburger buns out of the oven and replaced it with the baked omelet that had been chilling in the refrigerator overnight.

By the time she put the muffins into the second oven to bake, I heard Montgomery coming down the stairs and voices from the dining room as he greeted someone.

"I had better head out to see to our guests." I pulled my apron off and hung it from its hook. "How long until breakfast?"

"The casserole will be ready in about forty minutes. I'll run the bread and buns down to the café while it bakes."

When I reached the dining room, Montgomery had disappeared, but Clara was standing in the middle of the floor. I had never seen someone wring their hands before, but that's the only way to describe what Clara was doing.

"Oh, Emma, I'm so glad to see you." She almost ran to me and grabbed my hand, pulling me toward the front door. "Rose took Thatcher out for his walk, even though I tried to dissuade her. She insisted, so I told her to wait until I fetched my sweater, and I would join her. But when I came back, she had left."

I tried to put the pieces together. "I heard Montgomery's voice. Did he go after her?"

"Yes, but neither of us know which direction she went. He went toward town, and I'm to call the deputy and tell him to go up the road to the forest."

"Cal was going into Rapid City this morning, so you might not be able to reach him." I set my coffee cup on the reception desk. "I'll go up toward the mine, and Cal can catch up with me once he gets here."

"I wasn't sure if it was an emergency or not. Rose walks her dog every morning."

"But there isn't a murderer on the loose every morning. Don't worry. We'll find her."

By the time I reached the end of the driveway, I was wishing I had taken the time to grab my jacket. The morning air was chilly. I crossed my arms to ward off the chill, and walked up the road, scanning ahead for any sign of Rose. I was about halfway to the Forest Service gate when I saw Thatcher coming toward me. I broke into a run to intercept him.

"Where did you come from?"

Thatcher jumped up on my knees, his eyes showing white rings. Then he sat at my feet.

"Where is Rose?"

The little dog looked behind him, up the road. Had she hurt herself on the trail up there? Had she sent Thatcher to bring help? I mentally shook myself. This wasn't an episode of Lassie, but Thatcher was a smart dog.

"Thatcher, take me to Rose."

His ears turned toward me, and he stared into my eyes as if he was willing me to understand. Then he woofed and took off. I had to run to keep up with him. He ran up the road, and then turned onto the trail toward the mine. When we reached the entrance, Thatcher ran into the mine ahead of me, barking as he went.

I took my cell phone out of my back pocket and turned on the flashlight. I followed Thatcher cautiously. The mine had changed since I was last here with Becky. Rocks and gravel covered the floor, obscuring the rails in the center. I stumbled over the rocks, following the sound of the corgi's barking.

Suddenly, with a yelp of pain, the barking stopped. I heard a voice - a man's voice - and turned off my light. What was Sam doing here? My stomach churned as I crept down the tunnel. As I rounded the bend toward what had been the end of the mine, I saw a faint glow.

Hadn't there been a wall of rocks there when Becky brought me into the mine? The debris covered the floor, and I was climbing over piles of rocks now. It was almost as if someone had blasted through the cave-in to the tunnels beyond. But I would have heard something like that, wouldn't I?

Wait. Maybe I had. Becky had mentioned hearing something Saturday morning. I had thought it was thunder, but Wil said it might have been a poacher hunting.

Did poachers hunt in the middle of the night?

From behind the remaining rubble, I heard Rose's voice, bitter, but weak. "Did you have to kick the poor dog?"

"That mutt has been a pain ever since I came to the inn."

That was Wil. What was he doing here?

"Why are you doing this?"

"Because you wouldn't cooperate." Wil's voice was even more bitter than Rose's, and angry. "Just like my father, you refused to go along with my plans."

I peered over the pile of rocks. Wil paced back and forth inside a small open area beyond the rocks, a pistol in his right hand. When his back was to me, I lifted myself up a little farther. Rose sat on the floor of the mine, holding Thatcher's collar with her good hand. The dim light came from a cheap electric lantern on a rock, and next to the rock was an opening in the floor. That must be one of the vertical shafts Becky had told me about.

"What do you mean? We've always gotten along well."

Good, Rose. Keep him talking. Stall until Cal gets here.

"Well?" Wil shouted. "You think we got along well? You never listened to my ideas. Not once. And then when I offered to buy the inn, you refused."

"I didn't want to sell the inn. I still don't."

"If you had, it would have made things a lot easier. But no. You chose the hard way."

"You killed Dick Brill, didn't you?"

Wil kicked at a rock that bounced, then fell into the open shaft. It didn't make another sound for several seconds.

"He was being nosy. I couldn't let you find out about the uranium."

A squeak started from my throat, and I clapped a hand over my mouth to keep it from escaping. I dropped out of sight, but I was too late. Wil grabbed my arm, hauled me over the rock pile and shoved me against the rough stone wall next to Rose.

"And then you came." His hand shook as he pointed the pistol at me. "Always sticking your nose into my business. Making sure you're right there whenever Rose beckons. Falling over yourself to become her favorite." His lip rose in a sneer. "You make me sick."

I got mad. Fear for Rose's safety and mine gave way to anger at Wil's insolence. His cruelty. His betrayal. I started to struggle to my feet, but Rose stopped me with a hand on my arm. She shook her head as Wil continued talking.

"I had no choice. Now both of you had to go."

"You are the one who sent the threatening notes," I said.

He snorted. "Rose didn't pay attention to them. If she had, I wouldn't have had to kill anyone."

"You killed Paul, didn't you? And Mary?"

In spite of every cell in my body shaking, my voice sounded calm. Rose squeezed my hand. Someone would come soon. Just keep Wil talking.

"Paul? What a fake." Wil laughed, the derision echoing through the mine. "He found the uranium the first time he came up here, and when he found out about the mining deal I had made, he tried to blackmail me." Wil had been facing away from us, but now turned, his bloodshot eyes burning. "Can you believe that? Blackmail?" He gestured with a savage motion. "Thinking he could out fox me?"

He started pacing again. Where was help? It was taking Cal much too long. I shifted my position but stopped when Wil glared at me.

"Why did Mary have to die?" Rose asked.

He whirled away again, staring into the darkness of the pit in the floor. "She didn't. It was her own choice. She shouldn't have eaten the scone I had prepared for Paul."

Rose nudged me and jerked her head toward the tunnel leading out. I shook my head. I wasn't going to leave her here alone.

"Then the two of you." He broke off with a short laugh. "Hitting that tree instead of taking the straight route down the hill and into the canyon. I couldn't believe it." Wil clenched his fist in his hair. "What is it with you?" He whirled around, pushing toward Rose and punching each word with a thrust of the gun barrel toward her. His voice surged with hot vehemence.

"Why. Won't. You. Just. Die?"

That was too much for Thatcher. He pulled out of Rose's grasp, growling and barking. He leaped against Wil's legs, his teeth snapping as he snatched at Wil's hands. With a kick, Wil thrust him away. Thatcher yelped when he hit the ground but didn't pause. He gained his feet and jumped at Wil again, forcing him to take a step back, toward the shaft.

As Wil teetered on the edge, I jumped up to grab his jacket, but I was too late. The sleeve slipped through my fingers as he snatched his arm away. He windmilled to try to regain his balance, and then he was gone.

Sixteen

By the time Cal and I arrived back at the inn after Wil's rescue from the mine shaft and his arrest, Rose was in her usual place in the dining room with a steaming cup of tea in front of her. Thatcher was next to her chair, working on a large meaty bone. The breakfast casserole was on the buffet and coffee was brewing in the coffee maker. It was as if the morning's events had never happened, except that Becky was in the kitchen instead of Wil.

Cal pulled a chair out from the table for me, and I sat next to Clara.

She leaned over and said, "Don't you love it when we solve a mystery?"

I nodded, a little dazed. "And here I thought we were just trying to keep from being killed."

Cal brought me a cup of coffee, the Dark Canyon roast, and a serving of Becky's breakfast casserole. He had brought a serving for himself and joined us at the table. Becky came out of the kitchen and sat down.

"I suppose all of you want to know the whole story," he said as he stirred a generous amount of cream into his coffee.

"Do you know why Wil did what he did?" I asked.

"I spent the night following hunches. With Wil missing, my first thought was the same as yours, that Wil was a victim. But the more I investigated his background, the more I became convinced that these recent murders were just the next few in what might have been a life-long pattern."

"He has killed before?" Rose leaned forward.

"I wouldn't be surprised. Wil Scott was an alias. His real name is Scott Williams. He first came to light as a suspect in his father's death."

Rose shook her head. "He killed his own father? I never thought he would do a thing like that."

"The detective investigating the death suspected poison but couldn't prove it. And Wil inherited the family fortune."

"So that's where he got the funds to invest in the inn." The plot was becoming clear to me. "So, he was trying to get rid of Rose to get control of the inn." A puzzle piece snapped into place. "The uranium had something to do with it, didn't it?"

Cal nodded. "There is uranium around here in small quantities, but that wasn't a problem for him. He had salted the area with uranium ore, enough to convince a mining company to take an interest in buying the property. The only problem is that Wil didn't own the land, Rose did. The way the partnership agreement was written, if Rose died, Wil would inherit it all."

"If Rose was dead, Wil could sell the inn and the land to the mining company?"

"Then you showed up, and he had two people standing in his way."

"But Dick stumbled onto Wil's plans, and then Paul found out and tried to blackmail him."

"Mary was collateral damage." Cal took a toothpick out of his pocket and fingered it. "Finally, he decided to get rid of you and Rose before Rose could change her will."

"Because that would change the terms of the partnership." I stopped myself from chewing on my bottom lip. "That's such a sad story. And all for a few dollars."

Montgomery tapped the table. "Not just a few. Millions."

"Are we too late for breakfast?" Sam's voice boomed from the stairway.

I had forgotten all about the Nelsons. Now that I knew they weren't the murderers, I greeted them with a smile.

Nora followed him. "We were out late last night and I'm afraid we overslept. But we got a big lead on-"

"Shut up," Sam said with a frown. "The first rule is not to spill the beans."

"The first rule of what?" Montgomery asked.

"Treasure hunting," Nora said, ignoring her husband's shushing motions.

"Don't mind her." Sam pushed Nora toward the buffet counter. "She's all wrapped up in this story she's been reading."

"I've heard about buried treasure in the area," said Rose, also ignoring Sam. "Do you really think you have an idea where it is?"

Nora's eyes grew wide. "Yes, we do. It's gold bullion, stolen from a stagecoach."

I laughed. "Buried treasure? Are you serious?"

But I was the only one laughing. Every other face in the room was serious. Dead serious.

Just then, my phone pinged. I opened the notification from the inn's website.

"Good news," I said. "We have another reservation for this week. A couple will be checking in on Friday."

I set my phone down and leaned back in my chair. Even after all that had happened, we were going to have a busy week. Cal caught my eye and tilted his head toward the door. We left the others discussing buried treasure and went out to the front porch. Thatcher followed us, ready for a break.

While the dog went along the path in the rock garden, Cal turned toward me.

"I want to thank you for your help."

My insides were still quivering. How long would it be before I forgot the sight of Wil falling backwards into that mining shaft?

"I'm not sure I was much help. I was following the wrong trail up until the end."

"But you followed the trail. You didn't give up." He turned his hat in his hands. "I wouldn't mind if we worked together again sometime."

"Just as long as it isn't another murder investigation."

"Hey, how many murders can there be in one small town? I think we've met our quota."

How many murders? I ignored the queasy feeling in my stomach, but Thatcher had come back to join us and was looking at me as if he had read my mind. Then he winked one eye.

I shook my head at him. My imagination was working overtime again. The rest of the summer would be calm and peaceful, I was sure of it.

Jan Drexler

Author's Note

I hope you enjoyed your literary visit to the Black Hills! We have lived in this area for more than ten years, and every day I look up into those beautiful mountains and give a sigh of pleasure and thanksgiving. Sharing my favorite place in the world with my readers has been the best adventure yet!

This book has been my first independently published venture, and believe me, it has been a steep learning curve! I wouldn't have been equipped to take this step without the generous advice of writing friends, especially Ruth Logan Herne, Pam Hillman, and Pegg Thomas. All three of you are a wealth of detailed information!

I couldn't get along without a stellar editor, and Beth Jamison of Jamison Editing was great. You can reach her on Facebook at https://www.facebook.com/JamisonEditing Hannah Linder designed this fabulous cover. She caught my vision for this project, and I couldn't be happier with the results. You can find her at **Error! Hyperlink reference not valid.**

There are more mysteries planned for Emma and the crew from the Sweetbrier Inn. You can keep up with the new releases and everything Black Hills by subscribing to my newsletter. Head over to www.JanDrexler.com to join my mailing list.

You can find me on Facebook at www.facebook.com/JanDrexlerAuthor

Recipes

CRÈME BRULÉE FRENCH TOAST
Ingredients:
2 cups brown sugar
1 cup butter (two sticks)
2 tablespoons half-and-half or milk
 8 eggs
2 tablespoons sugar
2 cups half and half
1 teaspoon salt
1 teaspoon ground nutmeg
2 teaspoons vanilla
2 teaspoons Grand Marnier (optional)
 1 loaf day-old challah, cut into 1-inch cubes

Directions:
In a small saucepan, heat the butter, brown sugar, and 2 tablespoons half-and-half, stirring until the butter is melted and the mixture is smooth.
Pour it into the bottom of a well-buttered 4 1/2-quart rectangular baking dish* (about 14″ x 11″.) Place the cubes of bread on top, patting down if necessary to make them fit.
In a large mixing bowl, whisk the eggs, sugar, salt, nutmeg, vanilla, and Grand Marnier until thoroughly combined, then whisk in the 1 1/2 cups half-and-half. Pour over the cubed bread.
Cover the pan with plastic wrap and refrigerate overnight: at least 8 hours and up to 24 hours.
In the morning, let the casserole come to room temperature. Preheat the oven to 350°.

Bake at 350° for 35-40 minutes, or until firm. The edges will be puffy and golden.

Dust the surface with powdered sugar. Cut into squares and serve with warmed maple syrup or fruit – or both!

*This recipe can be cut in half and baked in a 9″ x 13″ baking dish.

MAPLE BACON BUTTER

Ingredients:

1 cup butter, at room temperature

2 slices bacon, fried crisp and crumbled into small pieces

2 tablespoons maple syrup

1 tablespoon bacon grease

Directions:

In a small bowl, combine all ingredients. Beat until light and fluffy.

Transfer to a serving dish.

Refrigerate leftovers up to one week, tightly covered. Or store in the freezer for up to three months.

Jan Drexler

Books By Jan Drexler

The Sweetbrier Inn Mysteries
The Sign of the Calico Quartz
The Case of the Artist's Mistake (coming late summer 2022)

The Amish of Weaver's Creek series
The Sound of Distant Thunder
The Roll of the Drums
Softly Blows the Bugle

The Journey to Pleasant Prairie series
Hannah's Choice
Mattie's Pledge
Naomi's Hope

Novella
An Amish Christmas Recipe Box, part of "An Amish Christmas Kitchen," a novella collection.

Books from Love Inspired
The Prodigal Son Returns
A Mother for His Children
A Home for His Family
An Amish Courtship
The Amish Nanny's Sweetheart
Convenient Amish Proposal

About the Author

Jan Drexler lives in the Black Hills of South Dakota where she enjoys hiking and spending time with her husband and expanding family. She has published several historical novels, including the award-winning *Mattie's Pledge*, and is excited to be starting a new adventure with a cozy mystery series, *The Sweetbrier Inn Mysteries.*

You can find out more about Jan at her website, JanDrexler.com

Coming Soon:

The Case of the Artist's Mistake

Sweetbrier Inn Mysteries
Book Two

Expected late summer 2022!

Chapter One

Becky thrust a mug of coffee into my hand.

"It looks like you need this."

I breathed in the coffee's aroma, feeling the brain cells waking up already.

"Thanks. I stayed up too late last night finishing that new murder mystery." I sipped the hot liquid.

Becky went back to filling muffin tins with batter. "Did you solve the case before the end of the book?"

"Of course." I took another sip. "What's on the menu for this morning?"

In the four weeks since Becky had accepted the job as our cook at Rose's Sweetbrier Inn, she had settled into the job like she had been born to it.

"A baked omelet and these blueberry muffins. I also made that fruit slush recipe Gran got from those Amish tourists last week." She slid the muffin tin into one of the wall ovens and set the timer. "We'll see how it goes before I make it a permanent part of the menu."

"You're using the guests for guinea pigs?"

"Don't worry. I tried it at Gran's and it's delicious. The guests will love it."

I felt the fog in my brain begin to clear. "Tell me again what we're doing this weekend."

"It's Paragon Days." Becky took the batter bowl to the sink and rinsed it with the sprayer arm. "It's a big thing. Folks come from all over the Hills for the parade on Saturday and the Ice Cream Social on Sunday evening."

"It sounds like some old-fashioned fun."

"Every Memorial Day weekend." Becky grinned at me as she refilled her coffee cup. "So, which float did you decide to join?"

"Me?"

"Sure. You have your pick. The church has a float, and Gran's Café is always a good one." She stirred sugar and cream into her cup, then her eyebrows went up. "Hey, maybe this year the inn should have a float."

"I don't know the first thing about building a parade float. And didn't you say the event is tomorrow morning? When would either of us have time to work on it?"

Becky slumped against the counter. "You're right." Then her face brightened. "But we can start making plans for next year, can't we? Do you think Rose would pay for some decorations?"

I laughed at Becky's enthusiasm. "Let's get back to this year. Are you still planning to go into town with me today? I want to distribute those new brochures."

"Let's have lunch at the café, then we'll do the tour. Most of the seasonal stores are open now. Except…" She left the word hanging when the oven timer rang.

I waited while she took the casserole out and set it on the counter. "Except what?"

"Have you seen the new art gallery yet?"

"The storefront across from Gran's Café? Don't you like it?"

She poured herself a fresh cup of coffee. "Hey, I like purple as much as the next person. Maybe more. But that place is-"

"Funky? Groovy? Way out there?"

"Yeah. Like something from the 1960's. And the woman who runs it is driving everyone in town crazy."

"She's new. Maybe people just need to get used to her."

Becky gave me a sideways look. "You haven't met her, have you?"

"She can't be that bad." I finished my coffee, feeling better already.

"She wanted Gran to paint the café to match her art gallery."

I laughed. "I can't see that happening." Gran's Café was firmly ensconced in its original mid-twentieth-century diner décor, inside and out.

"Yeah. Neither could Gran. They had words over it. Gran kicked her out of the café."

"Gran? But she gets along with everyone."

"Not Caro Lewis. I just hope the two of them can ignore each other for the summer."

I put my empty coffee cup in the dishwasher. "It's time to start the coffee for the guests."

"We have eight for breakfast this morning?"

"Yes. There's a family from Pennsylvania checking in this afternoon and another couple from Minnesota, so tomorrow morning there will be a full house."

Becky opened her laptop and started making notes. "Does the family have young children?"

"I don't think so. Mrs. Thomas asked about our wifi for her daughters."

"Too bad. I found some great kid-friendly breakfast recipes that I'm anxious to try."

"One of the reservations for the middle June asked about a crib."

Becky did a fist pump. "Yes! Little kids! They're the best."

"Let's just take care of this week's guests first. It's past time for me to get to work."

By the time I had the coffee brewing in the dining room, Rose had come out of her suite with Thatcher running ahead of her.

"Good morning." I scratched the corgi's ears while Rose shrugged her jacket on. "How's my favorite pup this morning?"

"Ready to roll." Rose gave me a good morning hug. "And you?" She backed away and frowned as she looked at me. "You look a little tired."

I gave my aunt a gentle push toward the door. "I stayed up too late last night."

"Reading again?" She stopped at the door and turned toward me with a smile. "I'm the same way." She winked and took Thatcher out for their morning walk.

Just as she left, Violet and Charles Bishop came out of the Summerwine suite, located just off the dining room.

"Good morning." I greeted the elderly couple with a smile. "Breakfast won't be ready until seven o'clock, but coffee and tea are available."

Viperish Violet. I regretted the mnemonic that had popped into my head when they had checked in the afternoon before, but Violet's long, thin body coiled in her wheelchair reminded me of a snake. I would have to come up with a different mnemonic to erase that first impression.

Charitable Charles gave me a smile. "We thought we would take our tea on the veranda this morning. Would that be too much trouble?"

"Not at all. You can choose your favorite blend and I'll help you get settled. The deck next to the library is in the sunshine this time of the morning. Will that do?"

"That would be lovely," Violet said.

I had just gotten Violet and Charles settled on the sunny, sheltered deck when I heard a door slam on the second floor. Betty Ann and Sally Marie were on their way down the stairs. The senior sisters from South Carolina were staying in the Dublin Bay. I didn't need to use mnemonics to remember their names.

"It's too early for breakfast, isn't it?" That was Sally Marie, the older one.

"Look at my watch. It's nearly eight-thirty. Breakfast has been ready for more than an hour."

They clumped down the stairs. Both sisters had donned hiking boots as soon as they had reached the Black Hills, but I doubted they would do much hiking during their stay. Their flowing blouses over bright capris were a cacophony of color that reminded me of a swirl of butterflies in a flower garden. Large, showy butterflies.

Betty Ann spied me as soon as they reached the bottom of the stairs.

"There's Emma! Yoo-hoo!" Her voice rose even higher in volume. "We aren't too late for breakfast, are we?"

I met them before they reached the reception desk. "It's only six-thirty, ladies. Please keep your voices down. The other guests are still sleeping."

"Six-thirty?" Betty Ann's voice was as loud as ever. "How can it be six-thirty? Look at my watch." She held her arm up to my face.

"We talked about this yesterday, remember? The Black Hills are in the Mountain Time Zone. Your watch is still set for Eastern Time."

"Oh, my, she's right," Sally Marie said, turning to her sister. "We forgot again."

"There is tea or coffee, if you would like some. You could sit on the front porch and enjoy the morning while you wait for breakfast."

Betty Ann pushed past me, pointing out the French doors on the other side of the dining room. "Look, Sally Marie. I told you I saw a woman in a wheelchair when we came in last night, and there she is."

I was glad the Bishops were on the other side of the closed doors, but I hadn't reckoned with the sisters' determination. In spite of my maneuvering, they slipped past me through the dining room, and out the doors to the deck.

"Good morning," Betty Ann said, sticking her hand out to the couple. "I'm Betty Ann and that's Sally Marie. We're the Brooks sisters."

Sally Marie took Violet's hand and shook it vigorously. "Everyone thinks we're twins, but we're not. Mama and Daddy just loved me so much when I was born that they had Betty Ann right away. She's always been my baby doll."

Betty Ann picked up the thread even before Sally Marie dropped it. "We're from Oxford Springs, South Carolina. If there's anything we can do for y'all, just let us know. We love to help those who are less fortunate. Mama always said it was why God put us on this good earth."

Violet withdrew her hand from Sally Marie's grasp, her face red. I tried to detour the sisters.

"Let's get your coffee, ladies. Didn't you want to sit on the front porch? We still have a half hour before breakfast is ready."

It worked.

Sally Marie turned back toward the dining room. "Come on, Betty Ann. You can put in as much of the pink sweetener as you like."

Betty Ann followed her. "Oh, my," she said. "Look at my watch. Is it really eight-thirty?"

"We've been through that, dear. You need to reset your watch."

As the ladies went to the coffee maker, I closed the French doors. Violet's expression was stony, but when Charles leaned over and asked her something, she shook her head and waved him away. Her face relaxed as she picked up her cup with a shaking hand. Charles reached over to steady the cup for her, and she gave him a smile of gratitude. They seemed to have forgiven the intrusion.

I left them and went to help the sisters get settled on the porch. I had my work cut out for me during their stay.

Printed in Great Britain
by Amazon